SLEEP
in the
DUST
of the
EARTH

Other Books by Anthony Hains

Birth Offering
Dead Works
The Disembodied
Sweet Aswang
The Torment

SLEEP
in the
DUST
of the
EARTH

Anthony Hains

Sleep in the Dust of the Earth

Published by PCNY BOOKS

Cover design by Elderlemon Design
Book interior by Cover to Cover LLC

ISBN: 978-1-7323880-0-0 (Ebook)
ISBN: 978-1-7323880-1-7 (Paperback)

For my in-laws, who were not the inspiration for this story.

Many of those who sleep in the dust of the earth shall awake; some shall live forever, others shall be an everlasting horror and disgrace.

Daniel 12:2

SLEEP
in the
DUST
of the
EARTH

1

MY MOTHER-IN-LAW'S PASSING was an unsettling affair. She was only sixty-eight when she died, and she'd been completely healthy up until the last week of her life. Or so we thought. Turns out there was an undetected heart issue that caught up with her.

At the time it happened, I was relatively new on the scene. Runa and I were still young, in our mid-twenties, and Runa was expecting our first child. We'd only been married a couple of years and hadn't planned on starting a family so soon. But accidents do happen. Her existence was a prime example. Runa was an "oops" baby, born when her folks were in their early forties. Her sisters, Adele and Karla, were in their teens when she arrived, and they found her a bit of an embarrassment. It meant their parents were still *doing it* at their age.

"The apple doesn't fall too far from the tree," I said to Runa after the initial shock of the positive pregnancy test wore off.

She rolled her eyes in reply before swatting me.

Nearing the end of her first trimester, Runa was having a tough time. A lot of morning sickness and general queasiness.

We couldn't wait for the second trimester when all of this was supposed to end, according to other people. The timing of her mother's relatively sudden death couldn't have been worse. But death is never convenient. Neither are babies, I suppose. At least the theme of life's unpredictability was consistent during this string of events.

On the bright side, to the extent that you can talk about a bright side in situations like this, at least Gretchen didn't suffer. Runa's father had died twelve years ago of an unusually aggressive form of cancer that devoured his colon, rectum, prostate, and bladder. The end was nasty, evidently. I still cringe thinking about it, and I only heard about the poor guy's downward spiral. From what Runa told me, her mother was quite stoic as her father was painfully consumed from within. She was constantly at his bedside, providing her full attention. She never broke down. Her father, however, looked haunted. And who could blame him. His body had seemingly rebelled against itself while he was powerless to intervene. Runa found his gaze disturbing. And he seemed to shrink away from his wife while she tended to him. It was like he became alarmed when she was present, or worse, terrified. My mother-in-law noticed this too and asked the oncologist about it. The doctor had no answer other than the obvious. He was in terrible pain, frightened of what would happen, and afraid of being a burden to the family. Anything could account for it.

His service was held in some way-out-in-left-field Unitarian Universalist church, which I realize may sound redundant. The family had been Catholic until Runa's father died, so her mother's conversion was quite something when it happened. Runa was in high school and stopped going after a couple of weeks. She told me that the congregation was full of atheist types, which meant the service was pointless. I mean, why bother going to church at all? At least this was her argument. Her mother gave in without a fight.

Runa's sisters were grown by then and Adele, the oldest, remained true to the Catholic faith. Karla slipped away from religion altogether and focused mostly on earthly rewards. The spiritual ones didn't offer the same tangible thrills. Karla's focus on social positioning didn't really gel until after she married Wayne, which was unfortunate since he was a car salesman. The right people didn't automatically think of him as upper-crust material, and Karla was seeing the world from the outside in just when she decided the best way to exist would be as an insider. Luckily for her, her father left a sizable estate that Karla could tap into. When a Toyota dealership came up for sale, she convinced Wayne that they should be the next owners. While Wayne was, unfortunately, about as bright as a low-watt bulb, Karla had more than enough brain cells for both of them. The dealership flourished. They hobnobbed with the right people. Relationships were brokered.

About the time Runa and I started dating, Wayne, Karla, and their two kids sold their cookie-cutter four-bedroom, two-bathroom house and "bought" the girls' childhood home. Runa's mother was still living there and ostensibly sold the place so she wouldn't be responsible for the upkeep. Runa didn't find out about the real terms at the time—after all we were in the throes of love and then planning a wedding. But later she wondered exactly how the whole thing transpired. Adele was no help. She lived simply and had no interest in the property or the subsequent transaction between Karla and their mother.

The house itself is really spectacular. Significantly larger than Wayne and Karla's old place. It's over one hundred years

old, Victorian, and impeccably maintained. I think it quali-
fies as a Painted Lady, with four different shades of blue high-
lighting the architectural details of the exterior. The inside has
all this wood molding, which creates a feeling of warmth that
doesn't exist in modern homes. There are scores of bedrooms
and hideaways. Karla's family of four and her mother could
roam around inside and not run into each other for days on
end. The place was that big.

It was also rumored to be haunted.

Its reputation was based, in part, on the architecture.
Ornate gables and turrets tend to ignite the dark imaginations
of children, and this house had plenty of these features. While
it sat on a large tract of land that kept the kids at a respectable
distance from the front, the back of the house bordered on
some woods, making it fair game for exploration and thrill
seeking. My in-laws were never particularly troubled by the
play of kids during the day, but they grew concerned with
the after-hours antics of teenagers. Occasional calls to the
police maintained a sense of order for the most part. But still,
kids being kids, some successfully trespassed and explored.
Legends grew about what was seen, and the rumors took on
a life of their own.

The lack of digitally recorded evidence didn't stop the
stories. And it didn't help that my mother-in-law started
dabbling in the paranormal around the time her husband died.
There were sessions with mediums and spiritualists. People
who shared her interests came to visit; séances, Ouija boards,
and tarot cards were occasionally involved. She never kept her
interests a secret, openly talking with neighbors and parents of
school friends about how she participated in the "scientific"
aspects of the efforts. People assumed she was trying to contact
her dead husband. While she never confirmed this, she didn't

discourage the talk either. It provided a rational explanation for her pursuits. Runa always thought it was something deeper, but never felt compelled to delve deeper into her mother's habit. Her "hobby" was positively humiliating for a teenager. She couldn't wait to leave for college.

Despite its reputation by the time of her death, I never had any strange encounters in the house, and Runa had a long track record of nothing but ordinary, earthbound experiences. Karla and Wayne never talked about anything remotely ghostlike, and they lived there.

Adele was a different story. She approached the place with trepidation, as if she could be exposed to some life-threatening contagion. The family occupied a permanent place on her prayer list, and she seemed to keep the house and its occupants under surveillance, watching for the slightest hint of the malevolent.

And then there were Karla and Wayne's kids. A boy and a girl. They were just plain creepy.

———

"I'm so glad you're part of the family, Ace."

My name is Jason. It was shortened to Jace by my younger brother when we were kids, and then Jace was shortened to Ace in the third grade. The nickname stuck, although adults continued calling me Jason. As I transitioned into my twenties, thinking of myself as Jason again was more of a pain than I thought it would be. Childhood friends and my brother still used the nickname. Runa was all over the place with what she called me, switching from one name to another depending on her mood. When my mother-in-law heard Ace, she stuck with it, finding it "charming." I liked her all the more for it.

"Thank you, Gretchen." Speaking of transitions, calling

my mother-in-law by her first name was daunting. She beamed at me as I sat across from her at the table, clearly not minding the familiarity coming from the guy who'd just married her youngest daughter. We were at our wedding reception and the DJ was taking a break from playing music. I took the opportunity to get off my feet for a moment. My wife—and calling Runa that would also take some getting used to—was still going from table to table and greeting guests.

"Runa is so happy," she said. "There's an air of authenticity about you."

I've been called many things, but *authentic* was new to me. I took it as a compliment and shrugged, not knowing what else to do.

"I'm serious, young man. True, honest commitment in a relationship doesn't always exist. But you have her back, as the saying goes. And I know Runa has yours. Some males don't display your level of maturity when they're fifty. You've got it now. A blessing, really."

"Ace! Kiddo!" Karla's husband, Wayne, slapped me on the back. Hard.

Gretchen smiled at her other son-in-law with an edge that could cut glass.

"So, Gretch, we've got another one."

Gretchen was never a "Gretch." She glanced at me with a subtle eyebrow lift that clearly referred back to her comments moments ago.

"Another what?" I wasn't too sure I was following.

"Man. To boss around," Wayne said.

Gretchen's lips pursed slightly. I felt embarrassed for the idiot. Even though her husband had been dead for a number of years, the comment still felt awkward.

"Now, don't scare Ace. You know I don't do that."

Wayne pumped his fist and growled "Ace" for some reason. And then slapped my back again. At that moment his kids appeared on either side of him. They snickered at the mention my name. The boy brought the back of his hand to his mouth and made a fart sound.

"You two rascals, come here," Gretchen scolded, but they knew she wasn't really mad. They scampered to sit next to her, and she draped her arms over their shoulders and pulled them in for a giant hug.

"My grandbabies."

The boy, Oliver, made another fart sound in reply.

"Now these two are my special treasures. They're angels." Gretchen kissed the crowns of their heads in turn, starting with Oliver's sister, Brinn. While the little girl gazed lovingly at her grandma, Oliver rolled his eyes. Even so, he snuggled in closer to maximize physical contact.

Oliver was eight. He had a sturdy upper torso that indicated a future high school football player, like his dad. His chestnut hair hadn't seen a comb or brush in hours, and his shirttail had probably been untucked for just as long. It waved in the breeze that accompanied his every movement. Brinn, six, was skinnier but by no means delicate. While she kept up with her brother, she avoided a rumpled appearance. Her dress was still crisp and her hair, the same color as Oliver's, remained in symmetrical bows.

I smiled at the two of them, but they didn't notice. Neither did Wayne, as his attention had turned to the shapely ass of Deborah Sully, one of Runa's bridesmaids. We both went to college with her and she was a good friend. Wayne's lecherous stare kind of irked me.

Wayne was a year or so older than Karla, so he had nearly two decades on me. Which meant that on any given day he considered me to be in the same age cohort as his kids. I'm not sure how this math worked for him, but it did. He was able to ignore me when convenient and grunt when he needed to be sociable. Thankfully, the football-cheer growl of "Ace" occurred rarely.

"You just have to tolerate him," Runa said after I met him the first time. "We won't be living in the same town. We'll hardly ever see him or my sister."

"Karla's okay."

"Yeah, well. She has her moments, too."

I checked out the room and noticed that Adele was standing as far away as she could from the DJ while still being in the same room.

"I do worry about her."

I turned back to Gretchen. She was clearly talking to me. The kids, still next to her, started to squirm. Wayne was still in the vicinity, his eyes scanning the crowd for another set of people to join.

I played dumb. "Who?"

"Adele," she said in a softer tone. "She's always been overly cautious... tentative. She withdraws from people too much. It's like she doesn't trust. I'm not sure where that came from."

"Has she always been shy?"

"It's not that, really. If it was shyness, well, you can survive with that. No, she tends to see the worst in people. It's sad."

I wasn't sure where this was going or how to respond. I looked to Wayne, but he didn't seem to give a shit.

When I turned back to Gretchen, the kids were quiet and unmoving. Both had leaned forward, were staring at each other. Oliver raised his eyebrow, and Brinn nodded. They leaned back and looked at me.

"She needs a conjuring," Brinn said. The boy giggled and

quickly covered his mouth. He glared at me as if daring me to challenge her appraisal.

"All right, you two. Enough of that."

Oliver still glared. "Okay."

I couldn't tell if he was replying to his sister or to his grandmother. "Are you guys having a good time?" I said.

"No." Brinn was quick with her response. Oliver smirked.

I decided to cut my losses and cease any further small talk with them. Gretchen made it easy for me.

"Oh, stop it, you two. You're just not used to fancy celebrations."

I thought this was a dig at Wayne, but he didn't react.

"Why don't you go look for your momma?"

That one Wayne caught, and he snorted. "Don't aggravate her now. If you do, you'll just get me in trouble."

The kids' faces became joyous. "Let's get Dad in trouble," one of them shouted, and they scampered from the table. As they tore away into the room, Oliver paused and picked his nose. When he wiped the contents on a piece of cake that was being cut, I jumped up to dispose of the slice before someone took it. Behind me, I heard Wayne chuckle.

I coasted over to Adele, who had joined Runa in a conversation with a former neighbor. Runa didn't know the neighbor as well as her sisters did. She was a teenager when the woman left the neighborhood and downsized to a small condo. She remained a good friend of Gretchen, and when I was introduced to her, the old gal—Mrs. Walker—proved to be an enjoyable storyteller.

"They used to enjoy their travels, your in-laws did. They went everywhere."

"Really?" I tried to keep up with all the banter as if I were fascinated with every kernel.

"Oh, yes. My husband and I, God rest his soul, got some of our best travel ideas after Gretchen and Raymond came back from their trips." For emphasis, she gestured with her hand. Liquid sloshed over the rim of the half-filled wine glass she was holding and landed on my shoe. She didn't notice.

"Gretchen could tell stories about the sites in Europe—they loved the Mediterranean. Her descriptions of the food almost provided a sensory experience. At times, I swear I was tasting the dishes. Of course, Raymond added the humor. He was always getting lost, stepping on animal droppings, or falling into water. You know, fountains, rivers, streams, canals. You name it. He even lost his balance once and stepped into a toilet." She chuckled at the memories.

Runa nodded enthusiastically. My smile muscles were starting to hurt, but I genuinely laughed at this report.

"Their last trip, right before he got sick, Dad got lost in Casablanca."

"I think it was Marrakesh, dear," said Mrs. Walker.

"Oh, yeah, maybe it was. Anyhow, he was in some marketplace and got off the beaten path. He ended up in some less tourist-friendly neighborhood. Buildings close together, dark alleyways, stares from the residents. Somehow he made it back, but when he did, Mom said he was white as a sheet."

Mrs. Walker was nodding. "And he said something like, 'Oh my, I felt like I was in a foreign county.'"

"Right, and Mom goes, 'Well, you are, dear. What should we do for dinner?'"

Both women laughed. Then Runa stared at something only she could see. "I miss him, you know? I wish he could have been here."

"I know, sweetheart. He'd be very proud of you. And happy, too."

———

Gretchen's funeral service was interesting to say the least. There was a eulogy provided by one of her friends, a longtime friend who talked about roads traveled on the journey and intrapsychic connections with humanity. The three daughters each said something. Runa talked about how her mother taught her to cherish the uniqueness in every individual. There were a few humorous anecdotes and a few hymns, and the presiding minister said some kind words. The service had no format that I could recognize. I guess I was used to the handful of really formal Catholic funeral Masses I had attended.

Karla's kids were bored to death. They sat limply in their seats and looked brain-dead during the speeches. Karla was glancing at the attendees to see who was there, or possibly checking to see who was noticing *her*.

Wayne, the dick, actually had his cell phone out, reading and sending texts. Runa briefly rolled her eyes at him before returning her attention to the current speaker. Her gaze became distant as the comments sparked her own wistful memories.

Adele looked troubled, and I felt sorry for her. Her motions were jerky, as if her whole body was about to erupt in panic. Her anxiety was nearly tangible. I would have liked to help, but I didn't know how.

A general wave of relief seemed to wash over the extended family at the end of the service. This included Runa and me, primarily because she was having another wave of queasiness.

Luckily for everyone, the visitation had been held the evening before and also an hour before the service. There was no gravesite service afterward as Gretchen had been cremated, so the family was able to bolt after receiving the last-minute well-wishers.

Wayne carried the cremains out to the car, with the kids in tow. They were fascinated with the idea that their grandmother was now a pile of ashes in a plastic bag placed within a container. I expected an urn, but the family—meaning Karla—opted for the more functional wooden box. I liked it, to be honest. The box was made of some kind of blond wood, so it was light brown. The edges were slightly rounded, and the lid snapped shut.

I knew about the lid snapping because when an adult wasn't holding the box, the kids would take turns sneaking peeks into it. They never closed it gently. Instead, they would let go, and the thing would shut with a solid slap of wood against wood. They found it amusing, but the rest of us were steadily becoming annoyed.

Karla finally spoke up about fifteen minutes after reaching the house. "Cut it out, the two of you. Sweet Jesus, you're giving me a headache."

After the customary whining protest, they gave up quickly enough. Still, they kept examining the contents of the box.

"Wow, that's Grandma," whispered Brinn.

"I know, I can't believe it."

I couldn't believe it either. The cremains didn't take up much space compared to the size of a human body. I expected a larger pile of dust, but what do I know. The term "cremains" sounded trendy to me, having never heard it before, like the death industry was putting an appealing spin on the whole thing. But again, what do I know.

The wooden container went missing about an hour after we got back to the house. The intent had been to place it on a shelf in the living room next to the cremains of my father-in-law, but it never made it there. I was the only person to notice. I recalled Wayne depositing it on the dining room table (and the kids continuing to check the contents). Then it was gone. I mentioned it to Wayne in passing. He shrugged as if it were no big deal. He assumed, as did I, that someone must have moved it out of harm's way after Karla told the kids to quit playing with it.

We were wrong.

2

THE WEATHER WAS fabulous later in the afternoon. I honestly couldn't recall what it had been like as we were preparing for the morning funeral service, other than not raining. By the time we arrived back at the house, everyone was commenting how gorgeous the day was turning out to be. The temperature was around eighty with low humidity. We all changed out of somber clothes and put on shorts and comfortable shirts.

Runa was still feeling out of sorts, if not as bad as she did during the service. She wanted to rest for a few minutes in the upstairs bedroom before joining her family downstairs. I knew this meant she would fall asleep and I would need to check on her after about an hour. Runa came from a long line of nappers, although she was a little embarrassed about this. It didn't bother me. I figured she was going through huge changes with the pregnancy, and neither of us would get much sleep in about six months. Besides, I usually spent this time reading or watching sports on TV—all without any guilt.

"Remember, don't let me sleep too long." Runa looked a little peaked as her head plopped onto a pile of pillows. Her chocolate-colored hair spilled over her face, which was decidedly pale for this time of the year. She liked working outside a lot more than I did and usually maintained a healthy tan mowing the lawn or weeding around the bushes, but the morning sickness had taken its toll.

"Don't worry. I'll keep the crazies in line."

Runa smiled and nestled into the bed on top of the covers. She stretched her bare legs and splayed her toes, a movement I loved to see. Her legs were one of the first features I noticed when I was jogging on campus six years ago and saw them striding furiously past me.

I stroked her leg and leaned over to give her a kiss.

"No, Ace. I can't."

"What?" I feigned innocence.

She smirked at me but then reached up and pulled my face next to hers. I received a peck on the cheek. I sighed out loud.

"Another time, mister."

I continued to change and wasn't surprised to see she had fallen asleep when I looked at her less than a minute later.

———

"Karla's got plans for this place."

That would be pretty obvious even to the least observant acquaintance of Karla and Wayne. I didn't know how to respond without sounding snarky. The best I could do was "Oh?"

"Yeah, she wants to bring new life into the house, or so she says."

Wayne and I were sitting on the deck in the shade while Karla rattled around in the kitchen. Her movements, typically orderly and organized, were frenetic. There was a lot of clanging and knocking. I had a feeling this burst of noisy domestic activity was a response to grief. Adele, meanwhile, was moseying around the backyard, checking out the land-scaping. She didn't seem all that focused on the shrubbery, though. I got the impression she just didn't want to sit and chat.

Wayne and I were nursing our beers. Well, I was nursing mine. Wayne was on his third. But who's counting? It's not every day you toast the death of your mother-in-law.

Wayne still had the annoying qualities of a frat boy, despite the passage of over twenty years and the addition of nearly thirty pounds. He was loud and sloppy when drunk, and overflowing with fake chumminess when not. His baby face was puffy and showing the effects of gravity while his physique was standard for a defensive lineman who hadn't worked out since his football-playing days at a Division III college all those years ago.

"What kind of renovations?" I suspected some kind of response from me was in order.

"I think the old gal was living with the original every-thing. Kitchen, bathroom, you name it."

I couldn't tell, not being an expert on kitchens and bathrooms. The water came on when you turned the knob, and we never lost hot water even with this crowd using the showers in the morning. Nothing leaked and all spaces were clean. Everything seemed fine. Then I recalled Runa's report last night while we were getting ready for bed.

"Karla's got all these ideas for the house."

"Oh?" This was always a safe response.

"Yep. Seems kind of tacky to me. But what can I say? She bought the place. Still, Mom hasn't been dead a week and she's already scheming."

"You're right. You can't say anything."

She threw a pillow at me.

"I mean, she wants to go with either stainless steel or slate appliances in the kitchen. That'll mean ripping out all the old stuff just because everything is white."

"Slate?" Did they make slate-colored appliances? What color were the kitchen appliances now? Funny how I never noticed that detail. She was right, though. They were white.

"They work fine, don't they?

"That's the point. At least she could hold off on announcing these things."

Anyway, with Wayne's "old gal" comment, I was able to recall this little bit of information from Runa to maintain my social graces.

"Runa mentioned that Karla wants to update the white appliances. Something about stainless steel or slate."

Wayne downed the rest of his third can and burped.

"Gross, Daddy." Brinn was sitting on the steps of the deck way off to the side. I hadn't noticed her or her brother when I came outside to join Wayne.

"Save the big pieces for soup." This from Oliver, who was a step below Brinn. They both giggled at the remark and then resumed huddling over something I couldn't see.

"Tell me you didn't think that up," I said to Oliver. "You had to get that from your dad."

"Who else?" Brinn replied for her brother. "Ollie, look. There's Snowball."

"Where?" The boy looked up and I followed his gaze. At that moment, I heard the tinkling of a tiny bell and saw a flash of white among the trees. Bushes shook in the wake of the movement.

"Ha. She must have been chasing a mouse," Oliver said. He returned his focus to whatever activity he was involved in.

"Here kitty, kitty, kitty," said Brinn.

Okay, so Snowball was a cat.

Wayne carried on like the kids hadn't said anything. "Yeah, that's it. Stainless steel or slate." He leaned closer to me conspiratorially. "I mean, who the fuck has ever heard of slate-colored appliances?"

I admitted that I hadn't.

"Anyway, kitchen work is on the fast track. A happy wife means a happy life. Right?"

I nodded as if this were a reasonable perspective.

"Seems like you already started with the guest room. That used to be Adele's old bedroom, Runa tells me."

When we first arrived and settled in the established guest room, Runa told me about its history.

"Her walls were pale lavender," she said. "She had posters that were reprints of famous paintings. They had titles along the bottom identifying the museum that owned the piece. I remember the Chicago Museum of Art and the Louvre."

I told Runa that I liked the color scheme Karla had selected for the redo of the room. It was some kind of lush green. I said the same to Wayne.

"Actually, that was me."

"You're joking."

"I mean, I didn't do the matching pillows, but I chose the color. Reminds me of golf courses in Scotland."

I could only assume that Wayne played golf in Scotland, although I couldn't recall him mentioning it. Then again, he didn't confide much in me.

"Well, it certainly fits. Good judgment. Maybe another career line for you."

Surprisingly, he laughed. "Could you imagine?"

A squeal pierced my eardrums.

"Brinn," Wayne yelled. "Quit that noise." He had shifted to the edge of his chair as if he was thinking about getting to his feet but stopped short of any further action.

Over on the steps, Oliver told his sister to shush and they both giggled. They were still huddled, and there was a magnifying glass in Oliver's hand.

"Brinn?" Wayne adopted a stern tone.

"Okay, Daddy," she said sweetly.

Wayne shook his head and sat back with a sigh.

"That woman got those kids doing the damnedest things."

"Who?" It was my turn to sit upright. I turned to look toward the steps. Oliver was inspecting something under the magnifying glass, or at least I thought he was. He was at the wrong angle to do it correctly. What was the matter with these kids?

"Gretchen. Our dearly departed. She was into this New Age bullshit. Witchcraft. That kind of thing."

"Are those the same?"

"Hell if I know. They were chanting and contacting spirits. Casting runes. Whatever. They were going to work on raising the dead when Gretchen got sick."

"What?" I'd had no clue. Then again, I wouldn't put it past Wayne to try and bullshit me.

Now the activities of the kids just twenty feet away were intriguing me. I stood up and walked silently toward them without intending to be sneaky. I didn't want to disturb them. At least that's what I told myself. As I came within a few feet, I noticed the tiniest puff of smoke.

Oliver was burning carpenter ants with the aid of the magnifying glass. He looked up at my approach, but just shrugged. He clearly didn't mind that I'd caught him in the act.

"They can't escape once Oliver has them in his death ray," Brinn informed me.

Oliver moved on, searching the ground and the steps for another victim. They were everywhere, it seemed, so the process didn't take long. Oliver lifted an ant gently in between his thumb and index finger. Its pincer jaws were useless as it wasn't in a position to defend itself. After Oliver dropped it on the step in front of him, he got the magnifying glass in position and focused the beam of heat on the ant. It scrambled to get away, but Oliver apparently had a lot of practice in remaining locked on his target. Within seconds, the ant was fried and a puff of smoke appeared. I even imagined a little *poof* sound. At least I hoped it was my imagination.

Let's be clear. I am not a member of Save the Carpenter Ants or a fan of insect pests in general. I would think nothing of spraying insecticide on the little bastards. But this seemed unsettling. I knew kids who did this when I was Oliver's age and I watched, but I don't recall ever doing it myself. It seemed too much like torture.

"Are you roasting them, Ollie?" Wayne appeared out of nowhere and looked over my shoulder. I was relieved because I wouldn't need to mention this to him. Did it qualify as one of those things that you need to report? I had so much to learn.

"Uh-huh. Frying their asses." He flicked the latest corpse over to a small pile of about ten others. Each was twisted and curled into a suspended state of agony. The grouping of the carcasses was ghoulish.

"Just don't set fire to the deck. Be careful."

Well, so much for Wayne's potential concern for his son's behavior. Or my ability to recognize unacceptable behavior in ten-year-olds.

I'd started walking back to my chair when I overheard Brinn mumbling. I turned and saw her muttering to no one in particular, looking down at the step. Her words were unintelligible. Oliver held a plastic baggie containing sand or dust in his left hand. With his right hand he reached in, took a pinch of the sand or dust, and sprinkled it onto the step where he'd tossed the ant carcasses. When he was finished, he rubbed his hand on his shirt and looked at me. He shrugged and attended to the sliding glass doors, which opened behind me. I turned to see Karla's head pop out from the dining room.

"Hey you guys. We've got some chips, dip, and veggies for appetizers before dinner. Want to come in and get some?"

Both kids yelled "Yeah!" simultaneously, scrambled from their perches on the steps, and rocketed through the open door and into the house. Karla called after them: "And help me carry everything outside so we can all enjoy them on the deck."

Wayne also disappeared inside. Birds chirped in the pleasant breeze while the late afternoon sun cast supportive shadows across all of the deck and most of the backyard. In the distance, I sensed rather than heard the small stream that rippled through the part of the woods that was on the property.

I toyed with the idea of joining Adele out back and actually took steps in that direction, but stopped in my tracks at the top of the stairs leading down from the deck. I had come to the location where Oliver and Brinn were engaged in their Junior Achievement efforts at sadism.

The pile of ant corpses was gone. Scrambling away in multiple directions, however, were about ten living, healthy ants. Well, most of them were scrambling away; a couple were fiercely attacking each other.

A chill started at the base of my neck and traveled down my spine.

What the hell just happened?

"Is the website business...lucrative?" Karla lowered her voice for the final word after the dramatic pause. She looked at me with the concern normally reserved for people talking about the survival rates of their stage-four pancreatic cancer.

"Depends on what you mean by lucrative. We're not pulling in millions, but Jake and I have landed some decent clients and the momentum is building." All of this was true, by the way. Jake was my best friend from college, and we both majored in computer science. We decided to go into business together. Things were slow at the beginning, which we expected, but Jake's dad had sent some business our way. Runa also had a job as a second grade teacher, which helped. We wouldn't starve, anyway.

Karla nodded like she knew what I was talking about. We were all still outside eating dinner, which consisted of a prepared deli platter with enough meat and cheese to feed an army platoon. Oddly enough, when we brought out the platter and two salads from the kitchen, we realized we were starving. Prior to seeing the food, nobody had been thinking about eating.

"Since Ace works from home, we're trying to figure out exactly how much child care we'll need once I go back to work," said Runa. She had woken up from her nap on her own. I'm glad she did, because I had forgotten that she wanted me to not let her sleep too long.

The deli dinner was exactly what the doctor ordered. It was simple and everyone could eat what they wanted. There was no mess or extensive cleanup, which fit well with the needs and the mood of the adults. I suppose the kids liked it too, but their antics made it hard to tell. They couldn't sit still. Brinn ate standing up. Between bites she would skip around the wrought-iron furniture on the deck. Oliver confined himself to his chair, but he shifted constantly on his butt while crossing and uncrossing his legs. He knocked against the table multiple times in the process, resulting in the sloshing of everyone's beverages.

"Ollie, for the love of God, sit still," said Karla after the umpteenth accidental kick of the table.

"I'm done. Can I go play?" Oliver stood without waiting, anticipating an affirmative response.

"Me too," Brinn yelled from the other end of the deck.

Karla relented quickly. "Just go, you're driving us crazy."

The kids scrambled from the deck toward the woods.

"Stay on the property!"

"Okay," Oliver yelled back.

"I mean it!"

"I said okay!" This from beyond the line where the trees started. The kids had already disappeared.

———

"I couldn't help notice your reaction before."

"What reaction? When?"

Adele and I were walking toward the woods in the backyard. When we passed from the lawn into the trees, I noticed an immediate change in volume. Once we were into the woods, the sounds of the others' conversation and the bustle of cleanup quieted to a whisper.

It was peaceful.

Runa had given me the evening off from kitchen duty.

There wasn't a lot to do other than bring the leftovers back to the refrigerator and throw out the paper products, so I didn't feel guilty leaving her with the task.

"I'm feeling a lot better, hon," she told me. "Go for your walk."

I had mentioned during dinner how I wanted to take a walk on the small trail in the woods. Evidently the family had an acre's worth of land back here. There were short trails that the kids played on while they were growing up. All led to a small stream that gurgled over rocks and debris and made a sharp turn before leaving their property to continue at a right angle until meeting a more substantial river about a mile away. A small bank developed over time at the ninety-degree turn that maintained a small pool of water except under the worst drought conditions. Ample rain had maintained the water flow over the spring and summer. The winter had been average for snowfall as well, and the surrounding elevations provided decent snow melt to add to the supply.

I had only been in this setting a few times over the three years I'd been in the family. When I strolled along the trails, I was always reminded of those old *Winnie-the-Pooh* cartoons and the Hundred Acre Wood. I'd been hoping for a half hour of alone time to get away from the jabbering, but when I was given the okay for my adventure, Adele asked if she could join me. I gave an enthusiastic "Of course," but I was sighing inside. Runa sensed this and gave me an apologetic shoulder shrug as Adele and I headed down the desk stairs.

"Give me a break, Jason." Adele was the only remaining person, aside from my father, who steadfastly called me by my christened name. Even my mother will gravitate toward Jace or Ace sometimes.

I had a feeling where she was going, but I didn't want to be the first to say it. I tried to look puzzled.

She took the bait. "You saw, what, the ants rise from the dead?"

Crap. Of course she would pose it as a question.

"Don't say you don't know what I'm talking about."

Okay, this made it easier.

"That was some kind of a trick, right?"

Adele shook her head. "You're like I was at first. Denying what went on right before your eyes."

"So, our nephew and niece have the power to resurrect the burned carcasses of carpenter ants. Talk about a curse for exterminators." I thought for a second. "Or a boon. This would keep them in business."

The shade grew darker as we walked due to a combination of the early-evening sun sinking on the horizon and thickening branches on the trees overhead. Ahead of us, somewhere nearby, we could hear the giggles and splashes of our young necromancers-in-training.

"You're not in the least bit troubled by what you saw?"

"Of course, but I figured there was some kind of explanation. Like maybe the ants weren't completely dead." I realized, even before Adele sneered at me, that this sounded really stupid. I was reminded of the line from *The Princess Bride*, one of Runa's favorite movies: "It just so happens that your friend here is only mostly dead."

"So, what do you think now?"

"God, I don't know. It was strange."

We made it to the stream, and the setting was as pleasant as I remembered. Somewhere along the line, the family had placed an inexpensive wooden bench atop an elevated bank under a maple tree. Adele and I sat down.

Oliver and Brinn had taken off their sneakers and were wading in the stream about thirty feet away. Brinn was doing a version of her deck skipping in the pool created by the elbow of the water flow. She tried to kick water in our direction to get us wet but came nowhere close. Oliver was being industrious, piling rocks to create an obstacle for the gently flowing water. The hems of their shorts were soaked, especially Oliver's.

"What're you up to, bud?" Adele called to him.

"Making a dam. But I don't think I got enough rocks to go all the way across." He barely glanced in our direction while continuing to forage.

"Careful not to drop one on your toes."

Within seconds of Adele's warning, he dropped a stone in the water and hopped up and down on one foot while holding the other. His repeated cries of "ouch" lacked sincerity, however, so we knew the demonstration was staged.

"Oh-oh, sounds like your foot is as flat as a pancake," Adele said.

"Let me see," cried Brinn.

Oliver flashed a disarming smile, and Brinn caught on.

They went back to their individual activities, and we sat in silence for a few heartbeats.

"Mom changed. I'm not sure how or when exactly, but I can remember a stark turning point." Adele continued to watch the kids. Her voice dropped, and I leaned slightly to my left to catch what she was saying.

"When Dad was dying, I took a leave from my job to come home and help out. Runa was still a kid, maybe in ninth or tenth grade. The whole thing was hard for her, and I suspected she and Mom needed the support."

Oliver sat down on the opposite bank where the stream

made its turn. His feet dangled in the water. He was gazing at a fist-sized stone, his blue eyes scrutinizing some detail on the exterior. Brinn scampered over and leaned against his hip. He showed her something, drawing a line across the surface with his finger. I imagined a cool-looking vein in the rock.

"Mom minimized Dad's condition. She had been telling us that he was going downhill, but slowly. Things were never *that bad* according to her. When I came home, I was stunned at how poorly he was doing. Mom had been keeping the worst from us."

Adele turned to look at me for the first time since we sat down. "He was in excruciating pain. Mom was maintaining her stiff upper lip, but I couldn't understand why she didn't give him more pain meds. I mean, at this stage, what was the big deal?

"I called the doctor and got the okay to do just that, and Mom was a little miffed, as if I were butting in. Which I was, but come on. Dad's pain improved and Mom calmed down. At least the awful moaning stopped.

"This was hard for Runa, which is understandable. She helped when she could, but she wasn't prepared for the groaning. Or the smell. There is a smell to the dying. Human waste and rotting insides—especially from the kind of cancer Dad had."

"Check this out, you guys." Oliver yelled as he strode over to us. The stone appeared before us with a flash, but he rotated the rock too swiftly for us to catch a glimpse.

I caught his hand and the rock to stop the motion, and Adele and I peered closely. The vein was impressive. It looked like forked lightning that circled the entire surface. I spotted the origin at one end and noticed how the vein extended and split off in multiple directions all the way to the other side.

"Cool," I said. "Looks like a lightning strike."

"Yeah. I think it comes from when the rock cracks and minerals fill it up. Then there's a lot of pressure squeezing it together."

I'd never seen Oliver so animated. His explanation made sense to me, as my knowledge about geology probably extended from some *National Geographic* show I could no longer recall.

"I wonder if there're others." He dashed off to resume his search. Brinn, meanwhile, had returned to dancing in the pool.

When the kids were out of earshot, Adele resumed.

"Not long after my father got his increase in morphine and had a couple of hours of good sleep, he told me an awful story. It was late at night, maybe midnight, and I was checking in on him before I went to bed. I thought he was asleep, but he startled me by grabbing my hand.

"He asked if we were alone and I said yes. Still, he swiveled his head from side to side on the pillow to see for himself.

"He said that Mom had put a curse on him. I brushed it off as a side effect of the medication or his illness. His voice became stern, more than I thought was possible given the cir-cumstances. He said I had to listen. Mom was changing. She was starting to believe in spells and such. He said he'd gotten this cancer in Morocco.

"By this time, my jaw had dropped down far enough to fit an entire apple in my mouth. I couldn't talk. He told me about their last trip abroad. They spent some time in both Casablanca and Marrakech. The trip was meant to help them work on their marriage. A few months prior, Mom found out that Dad had been having an affair and spilled the beans to us. They almost broke up. Mom was convinced this was it. They reconciled, though.

"Months later, they went on this trip to Spain, Gibraltar, and Morocco. By all accounts it was fabulous. We saw tons of pictures. But my father had a scary time of it in Marrakech. They were in the main square of the city to explore the vendors and watch the snake charmers. Dad somehow got turned around among all of the stalls and lost Mom. One of the vendors got hold of him and wanted to show him some jewelry. Dad reluctantly went along, thinking the man would ultimately help him. Instead, he was led through a maze of tiny streets. The residents stared at him as he went past, and Dad was worried that the vendor was going to rob him or worse. He was almost panicking when the vendor brought him to another stall with pieces of jewelry. Nothing jumped out at my father, mostly because he wanted to get out of there. But the vendor wanted to show him an ornate locket. My father opened it. There was some kind of moss inside. He rubbed his thumb on it and immediately felt sick. He thought it was some kind of narcotic. He dropped the locket, stumbled backward, and ran away, panicking.

"Then Mom was there, grasping his shoulders. He was only one street over from the main square, and he couldn't understand how that was possible. The vendor had lured him through street after street. He thought it was miles.

"They went back to the hotel, and he calmed down, and they were both laughing about it later during dinner. Still, he couldn't shake the uncomfortable feeling of illness as he recalled the texture of the moss inside the locket. Why would this vendor think he'd want to buy this for his wife?

"Three months after they went home, he developed a

sharp pain in his lower abdomen and groin. When it didn't go away and he went to the doctor, they discovered the advanced cancer."

A faint tinkling sound caught my attention, like a tiny bell. I looked over to where the kids were playing and saw a brilliant white cat approaching.

"Snowball!"

"Snowball, Snowball, Snowball," Oliver chanted.

Adele's forehead creased, and her glance shifted in Oliver's direction.

"I don't know where that cat comes from. Must be one of the neighbors'. I've never seen it."

"I saw it before dinner earlier," I said.

"See how someone tied a bell around its neck to warn the birds," Adele pointed out.

"So, that's why it's there. I wondered." I wasn't an animal person. My family never had pets while I was growing up.

Brinn was holding something out to Snowball. It was some deli meat from dinner. Had she been carrying it around just for the opportunity?

"Oh, shoot," Adele said. "They've been feeding the cat. That's why it's been showing up."

The cat wasn't shy about taking the food. But when it was done, it shook its head and pawed at its mouth before scampering away. The bell jingled as it disappeared into the trees. I wondered if it was scared of the water. I'd heard cats don't like water.

The kids resumed playing. It was getting darker. We would need to head back soon. I could tell Adele was thinking the same thing.

"This isn't the best stopping point," I said.

Adele pursed her lips and nodded. She leaned forward

slightly and turned toward the kids. "Hey you two, it's starting to get dark. You've got a few more minutes and then we're going back home."

"It's okay, Aunt Adele. We can get back by ourselves," Oliver replied.

"Listen, sweetheart. You really don't think I'm going to give up on my aunt duties that easily, do you?"

"Aww." This from Brinn. Oliver just rolled his eyes.

Adele resumed her account.

"Dad swore his cancer came from the moss in the locket. That it was some ancient Moroccan curse and that Mom arranged for it to happen. As retribution for his affair."

"You can see how he'd make these, what do you call them, faulty assumptions," I said. "He felt guilty for the affair. This trip was meant to help solidify the marriage. He was strung out on morphine and he was being eaten alive by this out-of-control malignancy. Who wouldn't come up with crazy ideas?" I felt good about my layperson psychoanalysis.

"That's what I thought."

"But?"

"He sounded lucid. I mean, as lucid as you could be with everything. He talked about the expressions of the locals as he wandered away from the square in Marrakech. They had judged him and found him lacking. He could see it in their eyes. There were whispers, he said. He couldn't catch all they said, but he heard his name, and Mom's name, and the word *adulterer*."

"Wait a second," I interrupted. "How would he understand them? They must speak, what, Arabic over there?"

"Yes, but French is also common. He knew enough French to get by."

A large splash and a gasp were followed by a ten-year-old voice saying "Shit." We turned and saw Oliver looking embarrassed. He was in the middle of the stream, leaning over the remnants of his dam. Some of the rocks had been removed and positioned along the bank. A bigger one was planted right between his bare feet. Clearly, that wasn't its intended location.

"I mean oops."

"You okay?" I asked.

"Yeah."

"You almost got your feet with that one, didn't you?" said Adele.

He couldn't talk his way out of this one. "It was close."

"What are you doing, anyway?" I said.

"Destroying the dam. I'll do something else with the rocks tomorrow."

I've got to admit that I was thinking about other possibilities for the rocks too. Like maybe a tower or a couple of bridges. Canal locks also came to mind. I could still think like a kid—it wasn't that long ago. This parenting thing might be kind of enjoyable.

"Uh-huh," Adele said. "You can see why I need to keep you in sight." No doubt about it, Adele could put a damper on a boy's fun.

"Anyway," Adele continued. "In addition to hearing these words, he had the feeling he'd seen Mom in the crowd. When he was panicking, he'd look around and out of the corner of his eye, there she'd be. Only for an instant, though. He'd search for her in the crowd, but she was nowhere to be found. Then she found him so quickly.

"He didn't recall any of this until after he calmed down. Some of it came to him the next day. He realized that it could have been a dream. Still, once he got it in his mind that Mom was watching and maybe somehow involved, he couldn't shake it."

"But how could she have engineered this?"

"Simple, according to Dad. She scouted it out somehow. Had a connection or made a connection. Through a guide, maybe. Or with the help of a hotel employee. Somehow she did it. The cast of characters knew who to look for and what kind of a curse to, you know, put on him."

"She'd have had to believe in this stuff. And known how to look for it."

"Exactly. That was his point. Mom did, or at least she was learning. Hence her growing interest in the paranormal."

I didn't know how to take any of this. We hadn't even gotten to the resurrection of the ants.

"Dad said that during his treatments, which were almost as bad as the disease, she would somehow inflict more pain. She would chant something over him. Once he thought she was rubbing him with more of that toxic moss. Whenever she touched him, the pain escalated or the spread of the disease accelerated. Dad had the sense that she was enjoying the whole thing.

"He was just emaciated when he died. Lost a ton of weight. He actually looked like he had an extreme case of anorexia. Poor Runa had to stay away. There was such a presence of death in the room.

"I talked with Mom about his comments. I felt guilty for bringing it up, but I knew he was accusing her directly. He had to be. I expected her to fall apart or become angry, but her composure was amazing. It was the disease talking, she'd say. Or the medication. We just had to take care of him as best we could."

"You guys ready to go home?" Oliver asked. He and Brinn

were standing before us with their sneakers in their hands. I hadn't heard them approach.

"Sure," Adele said brightly. "Let's go. Are you two thinking about dessert?"

"Yep, ice cream." Brinn took off at a sprint. Oliver was a few steps behind when he dashed after her.

Adele and I left the bench and followed. It was officially dusk now. The temperature remained warm, but the mosquitoes were appearing, making the woods a little less hospitable than earlier. I slapped one on my calf and missed another that was feeding on my forearm. I scratched the bite.

"Okay, what's the connection to Oliver's little show this afternoon?"

"Everything, I think. Mom's fascination with the paranormal went into full swing after Dad died. Maybe even before. When Karla and Wayne started having kids, Mom loved to babysit them. Karla liked the freedom and the help, and Wayne was fine with her shouldering a lot of his part of the workload. Then Karla and Wayne bought the house from Mom and lived with her. As the kids got older, they started gravitating toward her activities. She was thrilled. And she started teaching them. Karla and Wayne didn't see this or didn't understand. Or didn't care, maybe."

We broke out of the trees and into the backyard. Oliver and Brinn were many steps ahead and clomping up the deck stairs. Within seconds, they charged into the house for their dessert. Adele and I strolled more leisurely to the deck. She stopped and turned to me before we climbed the steps.

"I became more upset as time went on. I was concerned about Mom's becoming friends with a medium, or whatever she was. Runa referred to her as a witch. I met the woman, and she was very friendly. She didn't say or do anything disturbing, but every now and again Runa would tell me about a séance or other odd get-togethers.

"At one point, Mom asked me about raising the dead. I'm serious. This was around the time of your wedding. She'd become connected over the years with a group of women who'd developed weird ideas. I don't know if they were witches, wiccans, or devil worshipers. Probably not the last one, but it scared me. I couldn't help but think she was dabbling in something evil."

I waited for her to continue. We were still at the bottom of the steps. At some point, everyone would be wondering where we were, so I hoped she'd get to the end soon.

"I couldn't listen to it, so she stopped talking to me about it. But the kids seemed to catch on. Little things at first, then full-blown involvement. They talked about conjuring and casting spells. This past spring, not long before Mom got sick, I stopped by the house to drop something off. I forget what. I asked where everyone was, and Karla said Mom had taken the kids for a walk. It was after school and it was a nice day. I walked down the path and saw them. The three of them were completely naked, holding hands in a circle. I don't think they saw me, because Mom was focused on both kids and they seemed to be in a trance. Symbols had been drawn or painted on their chests. It was chilling.

"I ran, I'm ashamed to say. I wanted to confront Mom and bring it up to Karla, but never seemed to find the right time. I was also afraid. I still don't think Karla knows. She's too wrapped up in her own world.

"Since Mom became sick, I've overheard Oliver and Brinn make references to bringing things back to life. I shrugged it off, thinking they were trying to make sense of death. Then I watched the thing this afternoon with Oliver and the ants.

I knew you saw it too. Ants are one thing, but could it be worse? What if they've acquired an ability to do something more hideous than this? Something... unchristian."

Adele didn't look to me for a response. Her question didn't seem rhetorical, though. She started climbing the stairs as if she were seventy years old. I stood there flatfooted.

"Well, jeez. That's really fucked up."

Adele stopped three steps up and turned. I expected her to snap at me for swearing. Instead there was the tiniest smile, barely visible in the failing light. "Not exactly the way I'd put it, but yes it is."

"But... what do you want to do? I mean, is there anything *to* do?"

"I don't know. I really don't. I pray about it, but I feel like there should be something more. That's part of the reason I told you. I think you believe me."

I wasn't so sure of that. The whole thing was crazy. But I did see those ants. I honestly could not erase that from my mind.

"I need to think about it."

When the moment presented itself later, I told Runa about my chat with her sister. I had just gotten out of the shower and we were getting ready for bed. Runa asked if we could spend a few more days with her sisters before we headed home. I had no problem with it. I could work from anywhere and school for her was weeks away.

"So, what were you and Adele talking about?"

I didn't know how much detail to go into, but I couldn't see a downside to telling her everything. Out came the accounts of her father's death, her mother's interests, the strange behavior of Oliver and Brinn, and finally the Resurrection of the Carpenter Ants.

"Hmm," Runa said, as if she was trying to decide among entrées on a menu. "This does sound weird when you put it all together like this."

And that, as the saying goes, was that. Or so I thought.

———

I'd planned to go jogging in the morning right after I got up. I put on a pair of athletic shorts and a T-shirt and was making my way out the door when Runa grabbed me. Literally.

"Hold it." I felt her hand seize my forearm as I tried to escape the kitchen. The weather was great again and I wanted to get outside and do something normal. Besides, I had been sedentary for the past few days and desperately needed the exercise.

"Oh no. What?"

"We're going with Adele to search for Mrs. Baxter."

This didn't sound good. "Who?"

"Mrs. Baxter. The clairvoyant my mother was friends with from around the time when Dad died."

I groaned. "Oh, c'mon, Runa. Give me a break." This last part I whispered.

"Don't be such a big baby. You got Adele all worked up last night."

"I got her worked up? She came to me with the story."

Clearly Runa had been thinking about what I'd told her last night and talked to Adele.

So, off to find Mrs. Baxter.

"Don't get your hopes up, you two. I don't know if she still lives there."

"Sweetheart," I said. "I don't have hopes of any kind. I'd rather be working out." I was spread out on the back seat of

Adele's car, trying to get comfortable. Runa was in the passenger seat as we rode toward the west side of town. Adele may have had a conventional, cautious personality when it came to lifestyle and spiritual issues, but it certainly didn't extend to her approach toward driving. She was weaving in and out of traffic with the abandon of a race-car driver. Not a soul had passed us thus far, but we did plenty of passing. There had to be no police at all on our route. Either that or they all had broken radar guns.

"What do you hope to find out from . . . the witch?" Okay, I was being a little snarky.

"Adele and I discussed it. Maybe she can shed a little light on what Mom's interests were. Where she got the raising-the-dead idea. That kind of thing."

I kept my mouth shut, only because I couldn't figure out how we would bring the topic up. Assuming we'd find her.

"Runa remembers her a little," Adele said over her shoulder while keeping an eye on the road.

"You do?"

Runa turned around in her seat. "Yeah, I'm pretty sure. I was in high school and I remember her and Mom together a lot at the house."

"What was she like?"

"Friendly and kind of funny. In an amusing way, not a weird way. Although she was that too."

"What do you mean? What'd she do?"

"I mean, most of the time she wasn't weird. She and Mom would go to movies or concerts together. I think she was divorced, so it was, you know, natural that they'd hang out. Other times she'd be at the house having coffee. They'd talk about . . . whatever. When I was around, she would ask the usual adult-teenager questions. How was school? What are your favorite subjects? Do you like sports? What I remember most, though, was that they watched a lot of the same TV shows. She loved comedies."

"What about the weird part?"

Runa sighed. "It wasn't *weird* weird. The two of them read paranormal books and discussed them. Although, this would usually be with a group of people. Like a book club. The topics were strange. I didn't like to be around, so I would go out. I think there was a séance or something with the group one time. I spent that night at a girlfriend's house."

I didn't see the connection. "So, she wasn't involved with raising the dead." I said the last part with a spooky voice and made air-quotes with my fingers.

Runa gave me a look.

"What? You're looking for this person to ask about this, right?"

"Jason, this is serious."

I thought it was a reasonable question. At the same time, I didn't want to get myself into any more hot water. I tried to recast my comments.

"I am being serious. But, look, we're going to talk to a woman that you haven't seen since high school. How do you bring the conversation around to this...topic?"

"We'll start with telling her that our mother died," Adele answered. "Then, see where it takes us."

"It's not like we have to worry about her reaction anyway," Runa added. "This was a big part of her life. I think we bring up what Mom was talking about toward the end and see what she says."

I was dubious, but said no more. We were slightly west of town and the neighborhoods had changed. Gone were the older sections, replaced by newer developments. Some were fifteen years old, but others farther out were still being built.

"How do you remember where she lives?" I asked.

"We found her address in Mom's Christmas card notebook."

Wonders never ceased. "I wouldn't have expected that. I mean, that Mrs. Baxter would be a Christmas card type of person." Neither of them grumbled at me, so I guess I wasn't alone in my surprise.

We pulled up and parked in front of 127 N. Hawthorne Street. A ranch home that was almost quaint sat on the lot. While not ancient by any means, it was one of the older houses in the neighborhood. It probably had three bedrooms. An extension of sorts in the backyard—only partially visible—suggested a screened-in porch. That addition seemed more recent than the house, which looked as though it had been built around twenty-five years ago, out in the country by itself before the development sprouted around it.

I sat forward in my seat and practically pressed my face into the side window while inspecting the property.

"How old would Mrs. Baxter be?"

"She was older than Mom by at least ten years," Runa replied. "Maybe seventy-eight?"

There were three children in the front yard. Two were boys playing catch with a hardball. Both were wearing baseball gloves, and one of them had the stiff look of a brand new one. I'm guessing a birthday present he was trying out. A little girl rode a bicycle with training wheels up and down the driveway.

The kids didn't fit the scenario we'd all imagined. Nor, quite frankly, did the entire setting fit the demographic of a menacing old witch.

"Well." Runa didn't go beyond this.

A woman I hadn't seen stood up near bushes outlining the house. She had been weeding, going by the clumps of green she threw into a pail. She was probably in her thirties. Her strange-people radar must've gone off when we parked and sat at the curb staring at the house.

"Here comes the mother," I said. "We must look creepy. Her alarm bells are going off."

"Uh-huh." That was it from Runa before she opened the door and got out of the car. My wife's ability to spring to action is a lot quicker than mine.

"Hi," Runa announced as she stood. "We're sorry to bother you." She closed the car door. "But we're looking for someone who we think used to live here."

At this point, Adele was also out of the car. I was left sitting in the backseat looking awkward. I slid over, and forced my way out of the car. My legs were a bit too long for a smooth exit, so I must've looked, well, awkward. The woman assessed my threat level as I stood and offered my best disarming nod.

"Our mother died recently," Runa said.

"I'm sorry."

"And a good friend of hers was named Baxter. I can't remember her first name. I just called her Mrs. Baxter. She and my mom would get together a lot. This was maybe ten years ago, when I was still in high school."

"I was out of the house by then, so I didn't really know her like Runa did," Adele added.

By this time, the woman was nodding in recognition. Maybe we'd hit pay dirt.

"After our mother's funeral, when we were looking at the guestbook log, we realized no one had told Mrs. Baxter. Of course, we hadn't seen her for years. You know how life gets.

They were such good friends back then. We just thought it'd be nice if we tracked her down."

"No, she doesn't live here anymore," the woman told us warmly. The little girl was now standing next to her mother, looking up at us. I smiled, and she smiled shyly back and pressed her face into her mother's side. Score one for me. "We bought the house from her eight years ago. Our oldest was a little over a year old, that's how I remember."

"Aw, one of those boys, I guess," Runa said. God, she was good at this.

"Yeah, Justin, on the right. He just had his birthday yesterday."

So, I was right. New baseball mitt for Justin.

"We're expecting our first in February." Runa rubbed the tiny bump on her tummy. "This is my husband." She motioned in my general direction and I flashed my charming smile. My time in the limelight was a mere second. They returned to the subject.

"She went into assisted living. I think she fell and broke her leg. For a while we would get some mail and forward it to her. The place is over on Harvest Trail Lane. Gosh, I wish I could remember the name." The woman brought her hand to her forehead.

"Cherry Orchard Place," Adele said without hesitation.

"That's it."

"I drive by there every so often, that's how I know."

"I have no idea if she's still alive, sorry."

"That's okay. We can go check."

There was nothing more to say. We took our leave after we thanked her and the young mom repeated her condolences. There was no mention of the place being haunted or being visited by strange people in robes. Mrs. Baxter must not have left any strange vibes when she moved out.

As Adele pulled from the curve, Runa announced, "Well, we might as well go check out Cherry Orchard."

"Of course," Adele said.

I sighed quietly in the back seat.

———

Cherry Orchard didn't have that depressing warehouse vibe. Staff, residents, and visitors were smiling and chatty, and the place felt sort of like a country club. Mrs. Baxter's kids had chosen well for her. The male visitors, though, were all in pressed khakis and button-down shirts. More than one looked disapprovingly at my ratty T-shirt and old shorts. I really wished I were out running like I'd planned before being forced into this mission.

As we walked toward the receptionist, her gaze landed on me.

"That's the third dirty look I've gotten in the past ten seconds," I whispered. "I'm not exactly dressed for this."

"Shh," Adele said. "Just act like a moody teenager and we'll get you past the guards."

That kinda stung. At twenty-five, I was still carded in restaurants if I ordered a beer. My in-laws loved to point out how I looked younger than my age. Maybe forty years from now this would come in handy. At this stage of my life it was annoying.

As I'd anticipated, the receptionist was hesitant about letting a bunch of strangers waltz in to find Mrs. Baxter. Runa retold the story about her mother's passing and how her mother and Mrs. Baxter were friends. Since we didn't see

Mrs. B at the funeral, we thought it best to come in person to inform her.

When the receptionist asked for Gretchen's name again, I had a feeling we were in. Sure enough, Gretchen was on an approved visitors list. The receptionist relented and we were shown to the old woman's room. She was on the memory unit, as her dementia had advanced in recent years.

Mrs. Baxter sat in a wheelchair by her window, which overlooked a fountain. The room faced north, so the sun wasn't blinding. Instead, the temperature was comfortable and the view was calming. I stood behind Runa and Adele, who sat in the only vacant chairs in the room. Our excitement over being allowed to see Mrs. Baxter quickly deflated when it became clear that she couldn't help us.

Runa introduced herself, saying how she remembered seeing Mrs. Baxter at the house when she was a teenager.

No reaction.

Runa followed with the news about Gretchen, and I was surprised when her voice cracked a little. I'd been wrapped up in the day's detective work and had forgotten how the loss for Runa and her sisters was still sharp.

Still, there was no reaction.

Adele heaved the Hail Mary pass. She asked about Gretchen's interest in the paranormal and whether she knew about her mother's interest in reviving the dead. It seemed over the top given the circumstances, but it didn't matter.

Mrs. Baxter never flinched. She continued to stare out the window. I don't think she knew what planet she was on.

Runa and Adele looked at each other. They looked back at me. I just shrugged.

Adele stepped away. Runa leaned toward the old woman and said, "It was good to see you again, Mrs. Baxter. Thank you so much for your time and your friendship with our mother." She followed Adele's path out of the room.

I had to step back to allow both of them to exit. As I moved to follow, I felt something clasp my wrist. I looked down and saw a liver-spotted claw appearing out of a frayed housecoat. I traced the arm back to Mrs. Baxter, who stared at me with a shockingly alert expression. Her eyes were a faded gray, like two old nickels. I think I gasped and turned, looking for my wife and her sister. They were outside the door, gazing back at the scene with opened mouths.

Mrs. Baxter tugged at my arm. I leaned over, bringing my face nearer to hers.

"She'll be back." Her voice was like the shrieking of a rusted door hinge.

I recoiled, but she held fast. In fact, she jerked me even closer.

She smiled raggedly and made a heh-heh sound. Her voice still screeched. I swear she sounded like a caricature of a witch. "Sometimes they come back angry. So watch out."

Mrs. Baxter released my wrist. Her gnarled hand fell to her lap and remained there as if she had never moved. Her expression slackened. She faced the window again. I don't think she was looking at much of anything.

———

I tried to act like what had happened was an everyday thing. My attempts at nonchalance weren't convincing. Both Runa and Adele pounced on me after we left Cherry Orchard.

"What did she say to you?" Runa was hissing, actually hissing, in my ear. She clasped onto my upper arm so tightly it felt like her fingernails had turned into roofing nails.

"Ow, Runa. God. You're hurting me." She loosened her grip just enough to ease the stabbing pain. She didn't let go, though. I half expected to see blood running down my arm.

Adele was less stabby, but just as forceful as she escorted my other side, her hand on my shoulder. I had a fleeting image of adults dragging away a recalcitrant teenager and remembered Adele's comments about me looking like a moody adolescent. Maybe we looked normal.

I shrugged both of them off and strolled as naturally as I could toward the car. There was a beep-beep as Adele unlocked the doors with the keyless entry. I scrambled into the back seat.

"I don't know what was more traumatic, Mrs. Baxter's warnings or being mauled by you two," I said when both doors closed. Adele started the car.

"Oh stop," Runa said. "What happened in there?"

I checked my arm for damage and found that a couple of fingernails had broken my skin.

"See, look at this. I'm bleeding."

"What did she say, Jason," Adele asked.

The unsettling nature of the whole thing was sinking in.

"Holy shit. I mean—Jesus. She grabs me, like you did." I said, gesturing to Runa. "Scared the crap out of me. She was strong, but her hand was like a skeleton."

We were still sitting in the parking lot. Adele had the car running, but she wasn't going anywhere. Like Runa, she had twisted around in her seat. I leaned forward until our faces were two feet apart. In the background I heard the hum of the air conditioning working to cool the interior.

"She said something like, 'She'll be coming back.'"

"Who?" Runa said.

I shrugged. "My first guess would be your mother."

"What else?" This from Adele.

I tried to recall. "That was even stranger. Something like they're aggressive when they come back or, wait...*sometimes* they are." I shook my head. "Then she warned me to watch out."

Adele frowned and shifted back in her seat. I sat back and tried to position my legs in the limited space available to me.

"Does that make any sense to you?" Runa asked. She was still turned toward me, although I think she was talking to her sister.

"No," Adele replied.

I noticed Adele's eyes watching me through the rearview mirror. "What are you thinking?" I asked.

"The coming back part is disturbing. I can't get my mind off the raising of the dead."

"Oh, man. Holy shit." I sat up again and banged my right knee against the back of Runa's seat.

Adele turned back. "What?"

I reached over the headrest of Runa's seat and placed my hand on the back of her head. My wife looked back at me, puzzled.

"The ants."

"What about the ants?"

I could see Adele nod out of the corner of my eye.

"The ants. When they were revived, most of them were crawling away."

"But not all of them," Adele said.

"No. Some weren't. They were attacking each other."

Adele tied it together. "The warning is that not all things that come back to life are nice."

We sat in silence for a second.

"This is really fucked."

My comment broke the spell. Adele admonished me for my language with a stern look before she backed out of the parking space. After a mile or so, Runa spoke up.

"Okay, maybe we're going a little overboard. Who knows what Mom was up to, and so what? Everything is third-hand information. Who knows what you two saw with the ants." She exhaled slowly. "It is freaky, though."

"You should've heard her voice."

"You mean Mrs. Baxter?"

"Yeah. You remember the wicked witch from the *Wizard of Oz*? She sounded like that, only worse."

"I can't get over her. She wasn't even aware we were in the room," said Runa. "At least that's what it seemed like. Was she manipulating us somehow?"

"I doubt it," Adele replied. "Maybe she has moments of lucidity. Maybe we triggered something about Mom and their interests. It might've taken awhile to bubble to the surface."

"And she only spoke to Ace."

"Maybe because I was the only one in grabbing distance."

Both of them nodded. It made sense.

"Should we talk to Karla?" Runa asked Adele. I was momentarily forgotten.

"I don't know. Karla is...she has her own world. I mean, beyond us. She never sees beneath the surface of anything. And she doesn't handle deep family things well. I tried to talk with her about Mom, and nothing doing. She takes the head-in-the-sand approach to crises."

We fell into a true silence for the rest of the ride back. I was feeling claustrophobic and needed to get out of the car, to move. I'd been spending too much time on my butt. As we turned onto the street where my in-laws lived, I leaned forward as far as the seatbelt would let me.

"Sweetheart," I whispered, "I'm going to go running when we get home, okay?"

She turned and smiled at me. "As if I could stop you."

"Well, you did kidnap me earlier."

Adele chuckled as she flicked the turn signal for the driveway. "Listen to you, Jason, you sound like a twelve-year-old."

"Pathetic, isn't he?"

I pulled myself from the tight confines of the back seat and led the way around back, just in time to see Oliver bound from the woods like a gazelle. He tore across the backyard and sprinted toward the deck stairs, cutting me off by a step.

"Beatcha, Ace." As he raced up the stairs, I noticed that his legs and sneakers were wet. So, he'd been playing by the stream.

"Hello, you guys," Adele called from behind me.

"Hi, Aunt Adele," Oliver yelled, and yanked open the back door.

"Hi, Aunt Adele." Brinn's softer voice came from behind me as she ran from the woods and stopped at Adele's side.

"What are you up to?"

"Playing."

"In the woods?"

"Uh-huh."

Runa entered the singsong exchange. "Ace tells me you like the little river back there."

"It's a stream," Brinn said.

"I know. I used to play back there when I was a little girl. Did you know that?"

"Uh-huh. Did you play the same kind of games?"

"I'm sure I did."

"Brinn!" Oliver yelled from the kitchen.

"What?"

"You want something to eat?"

"Coming," she called back. She tore herself away from her aunts, scurried past me on the steps, and went inside.

3

I ALWAYS LIKED to run. As a kid, I imagined myself tearing across lawns and sidewalks without my feet ever touching the ground. When I pictured photos of me running—which were never taken as far as I know—I envisioned me in the air with one leg extended and the other leg pushing off. I'm not sure why I got such a kick out of imagining this.

It was only natural for me to gravitate to it as a sport. I ran track in high school and college. I was never a superstar, despite my pictorial fantasies, but I was better than average. It was also the only sport I could compete in. I basically sucked at everything else. I couldn't shoot baskets, catch or hit a baseball, or ice-skate worth a damn. I liked to tell myself that my body type prevented any other athletic skill development. I was, and still am, tall and slender. Almost skinny, really. So that left running, which I didn't mind at all.

There were benefits to it. I was in great shape, and even though I had no upper-body strength, I worked out in the gym sometimes to keep myself well toned. A huge plus was virtually no body fat, though I was young enough that I could get away with eating all kinds of stuff and not gain weight anyway. My father has told me this won't last forever, and

I should start trying to eat healthy. He's built like me, or I guess I should say I'm built like him. Now that he's pushing past fifty, he frequently moans about the little pot belly he's sporting. It's not as bad as he thinks.

The main benefit of running is Runa. That's how I met her. It was in April during our freshman year at college. The day was one of those that make you think miracles could happen. After weeks of gray skies, drizzle, and damp cold, the breeze turned southerly and the sun appeared. The air was sweet, and buds were popping open right before your eyes. I went running as soon as I could. I felt like I could have gone for an hour or two longer, but it was getting late. Dinner and a history paper were waiting.

I slowed to a walk to cool down before I reached my dorm when a girl went flying past me. Her legs were graceful and beautiful. She turned briefly to call back, "Sorry." I think she thought she had cut me off or something. I fell in love with a moment's view of her face.

I was fairly clumsy when it came to talking with girls I didn't know. My typical response would've been to let her go, but something urged me not to miss this opportunity, and I started running again. She maintained a surprisingly brisk pace, and not because she was a girl—well, yes, because she was a girl. She was faster than me and had more stamina. Still, I kept her in sight for a good fifteen minutes until she finally slowed. When I realized I was going to overtake her within a few minutes, I had to decide how I was going to play this.

I didn't need to worry. She turned around abruptly and stood facing me. She stared at me as I jogged toward her.

"You've been following me," she said, panting a little.

I was caught off guard. I stopped well outside of her

personal space, wondering where this was going. I weighed a couple of rejoinders, but decided on honesty.

"Yeah." I was panting harder than she was, so this was the extent of my reply.

She crossed her arms and smiled slyly. I was becoming rather confused.

"Good."

I scratched my head and looked at the ground. Sweat dripped down my face. I wiped it away.

"You're not mad?"

"No, this is what I hoped you'd do."

Okay, now I was really baffled. "You did?"

"I'm Runa." She held out her hand.

I shook it. "Jason."

"You go by Ace, though."

"How'd you know?"

Turns out she had noticed me on campus. I hadn't seen her, which was embarrassing at that moment. She asked around and learned about me. Maybe I should have been creeped out. Instead I was astounded, pleased, and, well, aroused, by the whole thing. We started dating and we've been together ever since. There's something about Runa that knocked me off my feet. I realize this is cliché territory, but it's true. She still has that effect on me.

I never expected to marry within a year of graduating from college. When I announced to my family that Runa and I were engaged, there was a moment of stunned silence before the squeals of joy and hugs all around. I know my parents thought we were too young, but they were roughly the same age when they married. I'm sure they'd say that things were different then.

My brother just shook his head and said "Dude" as if I

were signing my life away. I wasn't bothered by his reply. This was something well beyond the bounds of his own understanding and personal plans. He came around, though, and performed beautifully as my best man. He'll be our baby's godfather as well.

I was reminiscing about all of this while I was out running. Somehow the strange experiences of the past few days had gotten me thinking about how we met. It probably had something to do with being thrown into a whole new weird family pattern. All families had elements of weirdness, but Runa's family won the award. And I was no closer to figuring out how to approach Karla or Wayne about what was going on.

"What do we tell them?" Runa asked me. I'd brought up the topic right before I went for my run, on my way to the bathroom in the upstairs hallway.

"I don't know. Maybe that their kids are involved with this weird shit." We were whispering to avoid being overheard even though everyone was downstairs in the kitchen.

Runa shook her head emphatically. "They know already."

"Really?"

"Karla's been hearing the stories from Adele all along. Not about raising the dead. We just found out about that. But starting with Mrs. Baxter and up through the kids' activities with Mom. Things like the chanting naked in the woods."

"Huh. She wasn't troubled by the rituals the kids did?"

Runa thought for a second. "I guess it is weird in a way. But you heard Adele. Karla has a head-in-the-sand approach to life. She wouldn't cross our mother."

Now I was confused. "Look at the stuff they did, though."

"What stuff? Adele saw them naked in the river once. Weird, yeah, but nothing obviously abusive. Then the kids talking about bringing back the dead. Kids have wild imaginations. I'm sure that's what Karla was thinking."

"What about the ants?"

"Well, what about the ants? Did you really see it happen? How would you bring it up? Maybe the ants were just stunned and revived."

"I think they were roasted."

"Doesn't matter. Can you imagine how Wayne would react? He'd just laugh or blow you off."

She was right, of course. What we had was insubstantial—old recollections, deathbed whimsies, strange stories, and implanted memories. Not a lot to hang your hat on. I could see one of us trying to put it into words and sounding crazier and crazier with each effort. I could see Wayne's smirk getting larger and Karla's fascination with countertops growing stronger.

I made a pact with myself that I wouldn't turn into a distracted or cynical parent. Not having any experience yet made it a little difficult for me to picture exactly how I wanted to be with my kids, but I didn't want to be like Wayne or Karla.

My run had taken me for a couple of miles through some neighborhoods and the downtown area. A few folks were doing yardwork or washing their cars. One old guy gave me an enthusiastic thumbs-up. I felt more energized and alert than I'd been since our arrival.

As I turned into the family driveway, I slowed to a leisurely walk. I planned to mosey around the property to de-sweat before my shower. A dash of movement ahead caught my eye. Snowball zipped across the backyard, stopped dead center of the driveway near the deck, and watched me approach.

When I got within fifteen feet of the cat, I sensed something was off. Snowball was stalking something, and given her orientation to me, her prey was right behind me. I turned my head, expecting to see a bird. Nothing was there. I stopped walking and turned around, curious as to the intended victim. There were no birds on the ground, or any field mice.

I turned back to the cat. "Well, what are you looking at?"

Despite being heated from my run, I felt a chill run down my back. The cat was staring straight at me. She had closed the distance between us by at least six feet while I was looking away. She paused. And crouched. Her hazel eyes had a predatory intensity that was unnerving. Her fur, a glorious white at the stream yesterday, was now matted with smudges of dirt. Dried patches of crimson spread from her neck to her left side. What the hell was going on?

I stepped backward, and that was all it took.

The cat leapt twice, pounced, and caught my right leg just above the knee, latching onto me. I found myself speechless with surprise. Somehow the cat pushed the hem of my shorts higher, and her mouth widened. She struck, sinking her bare teeth into my thigh.

That's when I moved. I yelled all kinds of curses and grabbed the cat. I yanked her away from my thigh, which tore in dramatic fashion.

Blood started flowing.

I couldn't throw the cat. She hung on and scrambled up my arm to latch her jaws into my cheek. This time I screamed instead of yelling. The cat stopped biting me and reared back—this time to lunge for a target higher on my face. She tried for my right eye, and a quick twitch on my part saved my vision. Her teeth sunk into my face just below the lower lid, and I felt the cat ripping the skin with thrusts of its head.

By this time, I was in mortal combat with the damn thing, clawing and snatching at its legs and body. As quick as

I'd get a handhold, it leaped and swiveled all over my face. I tumbled over my own feet and fell awkwardly to the ground. I couldn't brace myself and landed on my right side. My head thumped the lawn, and while the ground was soft the impact still hurt like hell. The cat was thrown off, though, and I tried to stand and run for the door. But the little piece of shit was back on me in an instant. This time, it was biting my stomach. Somehow it had gotten under my T-shirt. I yelped again.

At this point, I heard screams from the house and clamoring footfalls down the stairs from the deck. The marines were arriving, thank God. The cat briefly watched the arriving horde of humans and dashed away.

"Ace! Ace, what happened?" Runa was first to reach me. She lifted me up by tugging an arm.

"Are you hurt?"

I didn't know how to reply, so I just looked at her.

"Sweet Jesus." Adele knelt down in front of me.

"What the fuck was that?" I yelled. 'Did you see that?"

By this time, Wayne, Karla, and the kids had joined the party by the driveway. Everyone alternated between shouting questions and making gasping sounds.

I couldn't put two thoughts together beyond the *what-the-fuck-was-that* and *did-you-see-that* variety. I was shaking uncontrollably and also really embarrassed. I'd just been attacked by a cat and the cat had won.

Both Runa and Wayne lifted me to a standing position.

"Can you walk?"

"Yeah." I took a step and didn't collapse. "Yeah, I can do it." Blood was dripping freely down my leg and into my running shoe. My T-shirt had splats of red, which were expanding. God only knew what my face looked like.

Runa's expression was focused. She adopted her elementary-school-teacher look for dealing with crises. I felt in good hands.

"Let's get you inside to clean up."

Wayne was trying to assist by supporting me on the other side. I'll give him credit. Adele looked stunned and Karla was dumbfounded.

Oliver and Brinn were awed by the event. And unmistakably thrilled. They couldn't suppress their grins.

———

The next forty-five minutes before we left for the emergency room involved alternating waves of humiliation and outright panic. Runa got me into a walk-in shower and quickly discarded my grimy clothes. Blood started flowing freely, and I have to admit it freaked me out.

"I think you're gonna need stitches," Runa announced rather loudly as she pushed my head under the shower spray.

"I can do this, you're getting wet." Truth was I wasn't so sure. I slipped as I had gotten into the shower, and I found myself grabbing frequently for the safety bar—which, thankfully, was in perfect position to keep me from flopping to the floor.

Runa ignored me and lathered my hair. "You could probably use a haircut."

I sighed. My hair was a bit long, which I preferred. So did she, or at least that was what she'd always said. But this was the first time in our relationship that she'd had to wash it.

The running water stung my cheek and my leg. For some reason, the mess of my stomach wasn't as painful. The blood didn't seem to be clotting; the water flow and the streams of red circling the drain reminded me of the shower scene in

Psycho. I think it was also disturbing Runa, who picked up the pace.

The bathroom was like Grand Central Station. Wayne snagged a couple of washcloths and put them in the shower. Oliver even came and stood inside the door.

"Whoa, Uncle Ace. Cool."

Naked and bleeding, I had no privacy. At least the female in-laws didn't come in. I received play-by-play updates from Wayne about Adele's WebMD research. That I needed to see a doctor was a foregone conclusion given the garish nature of the three bites. However, Wayne also raised the ugly specter of rabies, which Oliver found doubly exciting.

"Man, you'll be foaming at the mouth and afraid of water. I can't wait to tell everyone."

Karla, meanwhile, was cleaning up the trail of blood from outside to the bathroom. Fortunately, the path we'd taken was hardwood floors and tile, so the mop-up was easy. Thank God it wasn't carpet, or we'd need to hear all about the pros and cons of new carpet selections.

Runa and I each had our own washcloths and cleaned up the rest of me in record time. I didn't notice at the time, but dear old Snowball had also sprayed me with urine. That completely grossed me out. I was not a cat aficionado, so I wasn't up to date on cat behavior, but my understanding of cat spraying was that it served as a way to mark territory. Was it marking me? And if it was, what the hell did that mean?

When I finished showering, I dried off with Runa's help, but the flowing blood didn't make it easy. I finally procured a pair of underwear, which helped my sense of dignity. Wayne, God love him, was super fast in securing bandages, gauze, and tape. He and Runa mimicked a field surgery unit and wrapped me up. Even Oliver helped by cutting tape.

Runa thought another T-shirt and shorts were a good idea, so she ran to the room and grabbed a clean pair of each. Then we raced downstairs. (Full disclosure: everyone else was racing; I went gingerly. Every step felt like I was tearing open one wound after another).

It was only on our drive to the emergency room that I tried to make sense of the whole thing. And realized that I couldn't.

That cat's fur had been pristine yesterday—a well-cared-for animal. But less than a day later, it was a mess—coated in dust and splashed with dried blood.

Sometimes they come back angry.

I started at the thought. Runa looked at me briefly but turned back to her driving.

Well, fuck me blind.

"And how old are you, honey?"

The triage nurse at the emergency room had to be sixty. She was one of these sweet old ladies who said sweetheart and honey to everyone. Or so I thought until I heard Runa snicker. Then it dawned me that she thought I was a teenager.

I sighed. "Twenty-five."

The nurse looked surprised for a second and then recovered. Her fingers clicked the keyboard in front of her.

"And this is my mother," I added.

Runa swatted at me. "Oh, stop it."

The nurse laughed, and so did everyone else. I was still bleeding, though, and the two of them rallied to get the intake process done quickly. With only two other people waiting—someone with a bad cough and a kid with pinkeye, I was ushered to the front of the line and escorted to an examination room moments later. Runa came with me, which only reinforced the idea that I was sixteen.

The doctor was efficient in his suturing after the anesthetic took hold. "I hate to play blame the victim. But were you harassing the cat?"

"What? No. I didn't even know the cat."

"I don't know anything about typical cat behavior. I wonder if this is normal," the doctor said.

"Well, it sure was for this one. Look, I wasn't bothering or threatening the cat. Came back from a run, turned into my sister-in-law's driveway and there it was. And it just attacked me."

"Really, that's what happened," Runa said.

The doctor nodded. He didn't say much else beyond providing instructions while cleaning things up after completing the stitches in my face, belly, and leg. When he finished with the last suture on the inside of my upper thigh, he looked at me and scrunched his eyebrows.

"I will say this. If I didn't know any better, I'd swear the cat was going for your eye and your femoral artery."

I might've told him about the eye—in fact, I think I specifically mentioned that. The other thing, though?

"What's the femoral artery?"

"The large artery in your thigh. The main arterial supply of blood to your leg. You sever it and you get quick, massive blood loss."

Man, that I didn't see coming. I swallowed involuntarily and the hairs on the back of my neck rose.

What a freaking mess. Then we got to the really fun part.

"When I asked whether you were harassing the cat? I was looking for an alternative explanation for rabies. Cats carry it. We often think of dogs or bats, but cats do too."

"We have to find that cat," Runa said. She squeezed my arm and shook it like she was mad at me.

"That would help. But there's a real concern for me. The rabies virus travels from the initial bite source to the nerves, then the spinal cord, and then the brain. After that you're history. Sorry for being so blunt."

"So..." Runa started. Then she seemed to get it.

"Jace, you were bitten on the face. That means the virus doesn't have that far to travel to reach the brain."

Crap.

"I recommend that we start the vaccination now. You said the cat was aggressive. That's a sign of rabies. Especially in a domestic cat, which is what this one sounds like."

"We just saw it the day before, and it was normal then."

The doctor shrugged.

I saw his point. The disease must've come on quickly, and why take the chance?

"This is supposed to be pretty aversive, isn't it?"

"No, not anymore. You'll get two shots today, and then three more over the next two weeks. In the arm, not in the stomach. It'll be just like getting a flu shot."

So that was that. I would get the first two here and resume with our own doctor when we returned home—which couldn't be too soon as far as I was concerned.

We sat around until they rounded up the first two vaccines, which didn't take as long as I expected. Meanwhile, Runa called Karla to tell them what was going on.

"They think it's possible Bluebell had rabies," she said into the phone.

"Snowball," I said.

"Ace has rabies!" Karla yelled loudly enough for me to hear. Runa held the phone away from her ear and looked to see if she'd accidentally set it to speaker. "You stay away from Bluebell!"

There were sounds of digitalized chaos from multiple voices. I caught shouts of "What?" and "Who's Bluebell?"

Runa talked over the frenzy. "I mean Snowball. The cat's name is Snowball."

"I mean Snowball. The white cat that bit Ace. Stay away from it," Karla screeched. The uproar dissipated quickly.

"How's Ace?" Karla was still loud enough for me to hear her over the phone.

"Oh, he's fine."

I smirked at Runa. "I got all these stitches and I'm getting rabies shots. A little sympathy?"

"Well, he is kind of a mess," Runa added. "He has all these stitches and he's kinda grumpy."

Sometimes I can't win.

From the cell phone came Wayne's booming voice. "Well, I'll be damned. Should we eat without them?"

I was astounded when I looked at my own phone—it was nearly six. I nodded to Runa, who was clearly of the same mind as me.

"You guys go ahead and get started. We'll join you after we're done."

Adding insult to injury, the doctor thought I should have a tetanus booster, and he gave me a script for antibiotics.

The entire ordeal, not to mention the trip to the pharmacy, left me starving. When we got home, everyone was sitting around waiting for all the details. I refrained from showing them the bandage on my thigh, but the one on my face was in full display, and my stomach was fair game. I tried to make it look like it was no big deal, which amused Runa to no end. After chowing down on the sympathy meal and a huge slice of banana cream pie, I realized I was exhausted. Runa tore me away from the crowd when she saw my eyes drooping. After a quick pass at brushing my teeth, my head hit the pillow. I was asleep within seconds.

———

Whispers.
"Shhh."
Whispers.
"Shut up."
I was waking. Eyes still closed, I sensed rather than felt Runa beside me.
Urgent whispers. "...conjuring..."
What?
A thump. "Ow."
I opened my eyes. The room was dim with a hint of light around the edges of a door. Daylight or artificial light? There was dust or powder at the foot of the bed. The tiniest bit. Did Runa powder her feet? That would be a first.
I rolled onto my back and felt the pull of a bandage on my inner thigh beneath my shorts. The tug on the hairs sharpened my perspective and brought me around to full wakefulness.
Oliver and Brinn were at the foot of the bed, looking sheepish. Although the room was rather dark, my eyes adjusted enough to see them clearly. Brinn raised a hand to wiggle a hello with her fingers.
Oliver stood motionless, glaring first at me and then his sister. He sighed and inserted his hand into a plastic sandwich baggie. He'd had the same baggie, or at least one like it, outside with him on the porch when he raised the ants from the dead.
"Oliver," I whispered, trying not to wake Runa.

"Shhh," he replied. He took out a pinch of dust and sprinkled it on Runa's legs, then resumed murmuring to himself. Brinn hung on every word. For the most part, the dust floated away, although some reached the bed—hence the powdery feel.

"Oliver, what are you doing?"

Runa moaned quietly and my attention was drawn to her. Should I wake her? Probably not, but these kids were acting strange.

When I turned back to the foot of the bed, they were gone.

Well, shit.

I sat up in bed and immediately felt sick. Not like I was going to puke or anything, but swollen. My skin was hot, especially around the stitches. As I stood, I imagined my skin splitting under the strain of movement. An unpleasant image of a bursting sausage flashed in my mind. I stepped tentatively, and when nothing spurted, I felt confident enough to walk toward the door. Still, the achiness of my body worried me.

I left the bedroom, making sure to close the door quietly. My last image of Runa was of her sprawled on her back with the top sheet crumpled around her feet.

The upstairs hallway was lit by gas sconces. I swear to God. It was like the turn of the century, and not the most recent one. Shadows flickered randomly as I moved down the hall. The wallpaper had a floral design that repeated in vertical strips. And the hall was long—much longer than what it should have been. A door at the end was open, and a slightly brighter light within cast illumination into the hallway. I passed rooms where doors were sealed shut. I didn't even bother trying to open them.

What was I doing? And, more importantly, where was I?

I leaned forward and peeked into the room.

An emaciated man stood in the center. Cotton pajamas hung on a skeletal frame. He was ancient with yellowing skin and wounded eyes. His lower lip was thrust forward in a pout, and I feared he was going to cry when we made eye contact.

"Oh," he said with a slight groan.

"Sorry. Did I startle you?"

He shook his head. "No. I didn't want to meet you under these circumstances."

The smell hit me then. A combination of shit and rotten meat. His pajama bottoms were caked with fecal matter. He took a step, and chunks plopped to the floor where they joined previous droppings. Some of the turds were flattened as though they'd been trampled under his feet while others had the consistency of mud puddles.

I took a step backward. "I understand. You don't look too good, Ray."

Even though I had never met him, I recognized Runa's father. I had seen enough pictures of him. The fact that he was taking dumps in his pj's after his death didn't hit me as strongly as the smell of the shit.

Ray tilted his head back so the front of his neck was taut. He moaned quietly, and it came out almost like a whisper.

"This is so painful."

I didn't know what he meant. "You still hurt?"

"Son, you don't understand. I am like this...in perpetuity. She got her revenge. How she knew, I can't imagine. The vendor. She arranged for me to meet that vendor. How?"

Vendor? Then it dawned on me. Adele's story from two nights ago. Marrakesh. Ray lost in the marketplace, lured deeper into the maze. A locket, with moss or something like moss. He touched it. Then later he was sick, with cancer.

"They transferred the illness to me. A trick. A curse. The malignancy relocated from one body to the next."

Three brisk steps brought the dead man inches from me. He grasped my shoulders. Flakes of dried feces floated down like ash from where his soiled hands clung to me. I imagined the shit being absorbed through my skin. I thought I'd pass out.

"Ray...I..." I tried to step back, but he held fast.

"She knew how to accelerate the cancer. She tended to it, fed, made it grow. It ate me."

Ray sobbed but no tears fell. His eyes were drier than a desert.

"Be careful."

"Oh for the love of God, Ray. Stop whining."

Gretchen glided into the room.

"Look at what you did. For heaven's sake. Ace is a mess now."

Ray retreated from me and his wife. I looked down and saw brown handprints on either shoulder. The pattern looked like the artwork of a six year old after mixing all of the finger paints together.

A wet washcloth appeared in Gretchen's hand, and she wiped the fecal matter from me with a vigor that stung my skin. Droplets of soiled water dripped down my chest and back. Gretchen took care of those as well with the rag and then threw a bath towel at me. I dried myself off and hung the towel around my neck for safekeeping in case Ray touched me again.

"Ray we've got to change you again. Come on. Look at this mess."

My father-in-law shook his head and whimpered, but he still unsnapped his pajama bottoms. They fell to the floor, followed by his underwear.

He was missing the entire package—and then some. It looked like some kind of an animal had taken a huge bite out of his groin and then came back for seconds. I felt lucky that I'd only been attacked by Snowball.

"Tragic isn't it," said Gretchen. She pointed at her husband. "He sings this tale of woe, but who was guilty of infidelity? And not once, either. I ask you. Does this deserve sympathy?"

Ray looked at his filthy bedclothes on the floor and said nothing.

"Listen, Ace. I loved this man, but he couldn't be faithful. Time and time again. 'Please take me back, Gretchen. I'll never do it again.' Like a fool I believed him. Repeatedly. Then, one time too many." Gretchen glared at me, daring me to disagree. I didn't. "Thank goodness for Rita Baxter. God love her."

Ray collapsed to the floor, his back flush with a wall. I had a bird's-eye view of the carnage inflicted on his body.

When Snowball dashed through the door to pounce on Ray and gnaw at his ravaged body, I thought I'd lose it.

"There's my babies," Gretchen squealed.

Oliver and Brinn skipped into the room and hugged Gretchen. Cries of "Grandma" were muffled as their faces pressed against her breast.

The kids released Gretchen and beamed at her. I was momentarily forgotten.

"What have you two been up to?"

"Making sure you come back," Brinn replied.

"And practicing," Oliver added.

"I'm so proud. Let's see what you've been practicing."

Oliver reached into his pocket and pulled out a handful of lint. "Okay, check it out." He dropped the lint, but the descent wasn't gentle like I expected. There was a plop sound when the mass hit the floor. Snowball turned and looked too, its nose and whiskers coated with chunks of flesh and drying blood.

The lint wasn't lint. Dead mice littered the floor. Three of them, but who's counting.

Oliver reached into his other pocket and pulled out that damn sandwich baggie. He reached inside for the pinch of the contents and mumbled something chant-like. He sprinkled the powder on the mice and returned the baggie to his shorts. Then he lowered himself to his haunches. Brinn mimicked him, and they watched the mice.

"C'mon, you guys," he said.

It took only seconds. The mice shook and scrambled to their feet.

Gretchen clapped and hooted. Both kids glowed. Ray didn't seem to notice, but Snowball did. She began her approach, hunched low and stalking. She leapt at the mice and captured two under her paws. Releasing one paw, she clamped her teeth on the head of the stunned mouse and crunched forcefully. Drops of blood flowed. The second mouse squirmed under the other paw. Snowball held tight, but otherwise paid it no attention.

The third mouse took the opportunity to flee toward Ray. I expected it to hide behind some furniture, but instead if jumped onto Ray's leg and ran for his wounds. It sniffed around what was left of his groin and started biting.

Ray could only sob.

"Okay, Snowball, give it to me." Oliver held his hand near that cat's face. The furry little shit dutifully dropped the limp mouse into his hand.

"We'll do him again later, okay?" he said to the cat.

By this time, I'd had enough. These people were full-blown psychotic—and two of them were dead. I was ready to wake Runa, get the hell out of town, and go back home. I turned on shaky legs and headed for the door.

"Ace?"

I turned back to Gretchen. She smiled, but there was an edge to it. I didn't dare say anything.

"Take good care of my girl."

4

I WOKE UP gasping for air as if I'd been holding my breath. Maybe I was doing exactly that, which disturbed me even more than the dream. I turned to see if I had awakened Runa and saw that she was already up.

What time was it?

The digital clock said 7:48.

I pressed my hand to my face to rub my eyes before jerking it away. The cheek bitten by the cat had a bruised feel to it and was warm to the touch. I sat up just as Runa slipped into the room.

"Hi babe." She was in her summer robe, drying her hair with a towel.

"My face hurts."

"Well, duh." She took off the robe, started to toss it to the bed, and stopped short. Instead she placed it on top of our suitcase. She wore panties but no bra, and I would have found this appealing under typical conditions, but today I felt weird and slightly achy. And more than a little freaked out.

She started to dress but stared intently at me.

"Are you okay?"

The shades were drawn, so the light was dim despite the

morning sunlight. She reached for a wall switch to turn on the light. Her expression betrayed her anxiety when she gazed at me.

"What's wrong?"

"Your face is swollen and your stomach is red."

I lifted my head and saw she was right. Shit. And it hurt when I pressed my palm on my stomach where Snowball bit me.

I pushed back the covers. "Oh, Jesus."

"Yeah, I felt that too."

Gritty powder was on the sheets at the end of the bed. Some was even on my feet.

"That's what woke me up. I felt like I needed to take a shower." Runa pulled on a T-shirt, which fell over her shorts.

So I didn't have a dream. Those little creepy kids were in here doing something.

I stood and winced. My thigh ached.

"Did you start taking the antibiotics we picked up last night?"

My vapid look said it all.

"For God sakes, Ace. I think your bites are infected." She led me like a child to the bathroom. "Get in the shower and clean them up."

I kicked off my underwear and got in. She was watching me just like last night when I cleaned up after the cat attack, her innate mother behaviors kicking in. I would have laughed if the whole thing hadn't been so alarming. We turned the water on, and I waited for it to reach the right temperature before activating the shower. In the meantime, I started tearing off the tape on the bandages. I started with my thigh and then went to my stomach. Runa helped me with my face. The stitched wounds were rancid slits that oozed cloudy white pus. Runa looked as though it was all she could do to keep from puking.

After a quick shower, we grabbed something to eat and went back to the emergency room.

The emergency room doctor on the morning shift thought my infections had set in rather quickly but shrugged off any major concern. I mentioned that the injuries came from a cat attack. I left out the part that the cat had recently been raised from the dead. I also didn't mention that the cat had been playing, dare I say it, cat-and-mouse with recently resurrected dead mice.

It was too much, and I didn't want to spend the rest of the day trying to convince a psychiatry resident that I had a good handle on reality.

So, back to the drawing board. The sutures were removed and the wounds cleansed with some sterile solution, then drained. Thank God for the morphine, or whatever it was that they injected me with, or I probably would've been leaping off the table with every touch. Then more sutures and an intravenous administration of high-powered antibiotics. Followed by a lecture on adherence to medical advice. In other words, finish the damn antibiotics.

We returned to the house a little before one o'clock. I was starving again. We ate more funeral food. I've got to say, people had brought over good, fattening comfort food. I chowed down and felt much better. Physically, that is.

I decided not to tell Runa about the dream—beyond the basics anyway. Initially, I'd been ready to spill the beans about the sprinkling dust rite that the kids were messing with. But while I was enduring the emergency room check-in procedure, I started thinking. It was possible that I'd somehow felt the grit in the bed while I was asleep and incorporated it into my dream. That sort of thing had happened to me before. One time, I remember dreaming about my fifth grade teacher yelling at me, only to wake up to the sound of the yells. Except they weren't yells. A severe winter storm was in progress, and the wind hitting my bedroom storm window was making a howling noise.

Could this account for what I saw in the dream? Sure, why not. Thinking this way made me feel better. And I needed that. I didn't like the idea that my in-laws were a sordid version of *The Addams Family*.

Besides, I was tired. My head started nodding at the table. The hydrocodone tablet I'd had with lunch was taking effect, and I sure hadn't slept well last night.

"Why don't you go upstairs and take a nap," Runa said.

"Okay." I didn't need convincing. I stood and walked toward the door. "What do you say that we leave soon?"

"Sure." She smiled. "This has been way too weird."

I agreed.

———

I vaguely remember Runa coming into the room to say that she had to go help Karla with something and that Adele was taking care of the kids. I think I mumbled enough to let her know that I got the message, then went back to sleep.

Thunder woke me up. I wasn't disoriented or anything, but the lack of light confused me. It was just past five and there should've been plenty of late afternoon light. Instead an ink-like blackness filled the room. When distant thunder rolled again, I realized that a storm was approaching.

I moved to a sitting position and noticed a note left by Runa on the nightstand. It said Karla had had a minor accident while she was out shopping. Runa went to be with her. Adele was babysitting, so I didn't need to worry about Oliver and Brinn.

Not that I was worried about those kids. I had a feeling they could fend for themselves. I was worried about me being alone with them in the house. Thank God Adele was dealing with them.

As if on cue, I overheard Adele's voice downstairs. Then Brinn was talking, and the only word I could understand was *Oliver*.

"We can't use Grandma's powder on your brother," Adele said, her voice trembling. "It's not right."

And just like that, I knew what he'd had in that plastic baggie of his.

Dust and powder and grit of some sort? Yes, it sure was.

He was carrying a bag of Gretchen's cremains.

Cremains that he was using to bring dead things back to life.

Sometimes they come back angry. Wasn't that what the old lady said to me in the nursing home? Yes. That was it. The ants were attacking each other. Snowball did a number on me. (Which meant, by the way, that Snowball had been killed by the two kids. Maybe they'd wanted something bigger to try and resurrect. Holy shit.) And one of the mice went after Ray's chewed body—but that was a dream, right?

Where in the hell was the box that contained Gretchen's cremains? I hadn't seen it in a day or two. I bet no one else had either. Oliver carried around his sandwich baggie with the stuff. But that sure wasn't all of it.

I got off the bed and felt pretty good. The infection was clearly on the wane. I wasn't tired and I felt focused and energized.

Time to find the rest of Gretchen.

I wanted my movement around the house to appear natural to witnesses. Anything that remotely looked like sneaking was out of the question. I stepped out of the guest room and paused in the hallway. Sounds and movement from downstairs told me that Brinn and Adele were still there. It sounded like they were in the kitchen. I think they heard me too; their conversation became hushed and their exchanges brief. Maybe they were trying to be quiet on my behalf—which didn't make much sense given that I was already up and about, but I didn't give it much thought. I wanted time to explore the upstairs. Oliver's room to be specific. But where the hell was Oliver?

As if it were the most natural thing in the world, I strolled to Oliver's room. I planned to knock on his door, and if there was no answer, go in. If he answered (or worse yet, if I walked uninvited into his room only to find him inside), I'd tell him I was searching for everyone. And pretend that I couldn't hear Adele and Brinn in the kitchen.

My confidence in this scheme dwindled rapidly when I reached his door. I leaned an ear close and listened.

Nothing. Not a sound. No shifting or rustling.

I gave three short raps. "Oliver?" I whispered.

Again, nothing but silence.

Well, shit. I was actually hoping for the kid to appear.

I tried his doorknob and it turned easily. The room was dark, just like the hallway. Thunder rumbled, this time considerably closer. The approaching storm slipped my mind. Had there been other claps of thunder that I'd missed? Was

I that unnerved about the prospect of snooping in a ten-year-old's room? And the implications if I found what I was looking for?

Knowing the answers wouldn't change anything. Besides, I didn't care. Get in, look around, and get out. I stepped into the room.

And, of course, was surrounded by darkness when I closed the door behind me.

I'm such an idiot. What was I expecting? Whatever little light there was from the hallway would be cut off as soon as I shut the door. I stood a few minutes to allow my eyes to adjust, and that only helped a little. The clouds were building from the storm, and it felt like it was ten at night. Lightning flashed. The moments of illumination helped me see where the heck I was.

They also reminded me that I had my own source of light. I pulled out my cell phone and turned on the flashlight. Oliver's room had built-in shelves on half of a wall adjacent to a desk with a computer on it. I approached the shelves and scanned the contents. A lot of books that impressed me. Ancient Greece, ghost stories, the solar system, the Civil War, airplanes—a selection you might expect to see in an intelligent, inquisitive boy's room.

Another shelf held models and dinosaurs. A couple of trophies. A baseball mitt. I saw a Samsung tablet and a cell phone. Expensive toys for a kid his age. But what do I know?

On the bottom shelf, comic books were piled in stacks. On one of the stacks it looked like Oliver had pulled out a comic and positioned a few others at odd angles. An open superhero comic was draped across the stack like an apron.

As if he was trying to cover something.

I crouched down, reached for the comic, and pulled it

away. Sure enough, there was the box containing Gretchen's cremation remains. The comics sitting on top of the box were few in number and only served to camouflage the container.

I considered digging out the box but decided not to. I'd keep it where it was until I decided how to handle this. I replaced the superhero comic that covered the front of the stack. It was time to tell Runa, but I had to handle this delicately. How would I explain sneaking around my nephew's bedroom?

I stood up and turned toward the door. When the light from my cell phone traveled along Oliver's bed, I almost wet my pants.

The kid lay motionless on the top of his comforter.

His T-shirt and shorts were soaked, and he had been splashed with mud. His forehead had a huge gash. Blood was drying on his face. A protruding bump at the base of his neck tilted his head at an odd angle.

And, oh, Oliver was also quite dead.

I'm not sure how long I stood there.

I was paralyzed with fear. I know that sounds cliché, but it's true. I couldn't move.

What finally pushed me into motion was the sound of Adele and Brinn reaching the top of the stairs. Their footsteps indicated they were headed this way.

Adele's voice sounded guttural, as if she was trying to talk while crying.

I had only seconds to move. I got behind the door where I hoped to remain hidden until I could escape. I couldn't explain to myself why I was afraid they'd discover me. Images of my dead in-laws from my dream—if it was a dream— and those kids raising the dead with Gretchen's ashes flashed through my brain. Then there was that fucking cat. Yeah, I was scared.

The bedroom door swung slowly on its hinges toward me. I pressed up against the wall, trying to flatten myself into it. If the door hit me, I'd be done. Fortunately, the swinging stopped well before it hit me in the face. The space was wide enough for Brinn to enter. For whatever reason, Adele squeezed through sideways. Did she suspect I was there?

The overhead light blazed an instant later. Brinn was already past the switch, which meant that Adele had flipped it on. So, no, she had no clue I was hiding there. I figured I had only seconds before someone turned around and spotted me.

I began considering explanations for my presence when a simultaneous explosive flash and breathtaking clap of thunder rattled the house. A second later the lights went out. I couldn't believe my luck.

I let my breath out with a soundless exhale to calm my shattered nerves.

"Maybe we should leave the door open," said Brinn. "What do you think, Aunt Adele?"

"What?"

"The door. Should we leave it open?"

"Sure, honey, let's do that."

God bless you, Adele. Although this might let extra light into the room.

A flashlight came on. Brinn was holding it. I couldn't tell where she got it. Maybe it was Oliver's. But what did it matter?

Brinn turned unexpectedly. The circle of light dashed around the room and landed on the door. Her tiny hand grasped the door and swung it open about two additional feet. The light swooped across my chest for a moment and then skirted away.

"We have to open it a little so Uncle Ace can see."

Adele gasped.

My heart sank. Brinn knew I was there.

"You're a silly guy, Uncle Ace." She turned back to the body of her brother.

Adele's face slowly peeked around the door. Even in the dim light, her eyes were like hubcaps and her face streamed with tears.

Brinn reached behind her back for Adele and shook her arm. She handed the flashlight to Adele. "We better get started."

Adele moaned, and the illumination from the flashlight trembled across the far wall.

"You gotta hold it still," Brinn said.

Brinn and Adele were visible as silhouettes and shadows. Brinn stood next to Oliver's bed and loomed over his midsection. Adele fell to her knees and looked as if she was praying. Her hands clasped the flashlight and her elbows were positioned at the edge of the bed. Her head slumped next to her raised forearms with her forehead resting on the mattress.

"Oh, my God."

"Aunt Adele, shush now."

"I never meant for this to happen. This is all my fault."

"Yeah, it is, but we can fix it. You shoulda let us kill you like we planned."

Adele sobbed again.

Brinn talked over her shoulder to me. "We were supposed to practice on Aunt Adele. Not Oliver." She turned around to face me. "We went into the woods and Oliver jumped onto the bench by the stream. Where you sat the other night? He was going to hit Aunt Adele with a rock. She stopped him, though. He fell. And he crashed head first right into one of those big rocks. It was gooshy."

She faced her brother again

"So, we gotta do the conjuring on him. I hope it works, don't you?"

"Dear Jesus, forgive me, please. I had no idea. Oh God, what do I do? I can't let him stay this way..." Adele's cries held such anguish that I expected her to keel over and faint.

"Stop it. We have to try this. I watched Oliver do it so I know how."

Brinn pulled the plastic baggie containing Gretchen's cremains out of her pocket. She opened it and shook the bag vigorously over Oliver's body. Powder flew in all directions, danced in the flashlight beam, and came to rest on Oliver, covering him from his knees to his hairline.

Brinn squeezed the empty baggie in her fist and tossed it over her shoulder. The bag disappeared in the darkness. I sensed that it had landed just a few steps from my feet. Adele quieted, but her shoulders continued to shake. Brinn began chanting something. I strained to hear the words, but they were indecipherable. Adele swayed with the chant as Brinn's intonation took on a singsong quality.

I thought of stepping forward and stopping the ritual. I really did. Let the legal process take over and the natural order of things unfold when it came to a death of a child. But I was frozen in place. Part was fear, yes, but part was fascination.

Brinn finished. The silence was abrupt. I heard the hitch of a sob from Adele. Lightning flashed, and the thunder followed with a clash. Rain splattered the windows, pushed by a gust of wind. Otherwise, nothing moved in Oliver's bedroom.

"Maybe it'll take a little while," Brinn offered. She didn't sound overly concerned. "Snowball didn't come back right away."

Adele whimpered in reply.

Brinn reached for the flashlight that was still in Adele's hands and scampered over to the bookshelves. The light danced chaotically as comic books spilled to the floor. When Brinn turned around she held the wooden box containing Gretchen's cremains. "We're out of that one baggie. We need to get some more."

Brinn strolled back to Adele beaming with a wide smile. She nuzzled Adele. "C'mon, Aunt Adele, it's almost dinnertime. Maybe Momma will be home soon."

"Oh." Adele's voice was in danger of escalating into a wail. "What'll I tell her?"

"Don't worry. He'll be okay. C'mon, let's go downstairs. You coming, Uncle Ace?"

I flattened myself against the wall behind the door. I couldn't respond.

"That's okay. You can keep watch. Let us know when something happens."

The bed creaked as Adele pushed off the mattress to stand on her feet.

I focused on Oliver, who looked as dead as he had before. From the corner of my eye, I saw Brinn and Adele shuffle away from the bed. Their footsteps barely registered as they moved to the door. A small hand clasped the edge of the door and pulled it after them as they left the room. I stood in the dark with the corpse of my nephew.

I exhaled slowly to help the tension leave my body, but my limbs were shivering. I leaned against the wall, slid to the floor, brought my knees up to my chest, and sat there huddled, closing my eyes to reorient myself to a sense of normalcy.

What to do? I knew I'd have to spill my guts to Runa. This would really throw the family into turmoil. A child, dead, possibly at his aunt's hand. It had to be an accident. Adele would no sooner harm this kid than slice her own throat. Still, the situation was horrifying. And when the occult mixings rose to the top of the family narrative, God only knew what would happen.

"Ace."

No way. But I had to admit, I wasn't surprised.

I kept my eyes closed. I didn't dare open them and look up.

"C'mon, Ace. Check it out. Don't be a shit."

I checked it out.

Oliver stood before me. Did I ever doubt this outcome? Yes? No? Maybe. I don't know. I couldn't speak. I swallowed involuntarily. I shivered and I wondered if I would ever sleep without nightmares again.

Oliver's shirt was still caked in dirt. Red splashes from his head wound splayed across the front. His shorts were in better shape, although they were damp and rumpled.

He wiggled his toes. The huge gash on his head was gone—as was the bump on his neck. The storm had passed quickly, and the sun was breaking out from behind the diminishing cloud cover. I could see the kid clearly.

"Remember what that old lady told you?"

I could only manage a confused frown.

"Sometimes they come back angry. Remember?" Oliver smiled but his eyes remained soulless. His teeth dripped saliva. Then he growled.

I closed my eyes again and waited for the attack. I wondered what he would do. And if it would hurt.

"But sometimes they don't." He giggled and gave my head a tap.

I dared to look, fully expecting a trick. But he stood there and smiled, like a mischievous ten-year-old.

"Later, Ace." Oliver opened his bedroom door and left to present himself to his sister. And aunt.

Epilogue

I MADE A decision I feared would cost me my marriage. I told Runa everything.

God love her, though. There was never any question in her mind that I was telling the truth, no resentment against me for holding these suspicions. She had pursued the investigation into Gretchen's occult practices, after all.

We didn't mention anything to Wayne and Karla. How could we? Oliver was his usual self by the time they got home that night. By then he had cleaned up and looked presentable. Maybe it was the irritation of dealing with the car that caused them to overlook any raised-from-the-dead nuances in their son. Then again, there really wasn't anything to notice. Oliver looked and acted the same as before his death and resurrection. At least I didn't see any differences. But I'd always thought the kid was a little weird anyway.

Adele assumed a degree of stoicism I would have thought impossible for a woman of strong religious beliefs who had recently played a huge role in the death of her nephew and then participated in his occult resurrection ceremony. I was the only one who could tell that she was this close to losing her sanity. She described the afternoon in terms of everyday activities—going into some detail about the ferocity of the storm—and then made excuses to take her leave and return to her apartment in town. One little anecdote of creepiness: during her review of the shared activities, Oliver came up and put his arm around her waist. I thought Adele would scream, but she carried off the rest of her narrative with barely a flinch.

We got out of Dodge the next day and headed home. There, we entered into a routine as best we could and prepared for the baby. The infection dissipated quickly, and I completed my rabies shots. Runa went back to the class-room, where she planned to stay until the baby came. She was looking at taking a month off and then returning. The strategy was for me to take over at home since I could work from anywhere. I was okay with the idea. After all, babies just poop, eat, and sleep. How hard could it be?

When I said as much to my parents, my father just looked at me and chuckled. But really. Looking back on my life as a kid, I'd say raising me was a piece of cake. Relatively speaking.

A month after the craziness with Gretchen's funeral, Adele got a new job near us. She was able to move out of her apart-ment with little difficulty and found a place only a few miles from our place. We were happy for her and welcomed her frequent visits with open arms. Still, something was missing. Her eyes lacked a certain sparkle, and she was a little more subdued. We couldn't quite put our fingers on it. She lost an important feature of her soul, and we're not sure if she'll ever be able to reclaim it.

Karla hated to see her go. Adele had always been a willing babysitter, and Karla reported that the kids missed her terribly. Oliver was becoming more of a handful, which she attributed to his approaching adolescence. We acknowledged this pos-sibility, although the three of us could envision other causes.

Speaking of Oliver, an incident occurred where a girl from his school disappeared without a trace. She was found two days later along the road not far from Karla and Wayne's place. Found by Oliver. At least that was the report from the police and in the news. No one saw the discovery, and the girl couldn't remember anything that had happened when she was missing. The police were treating it like an abduction, since she seemed to have suffered some kind of trauma. This was echoed by the girl's parents, who reported that the girl was very aggressive after returning to the family. She even injured her baby brother. Karla was so pleased to have a son who was a hero.

I couldn't help wondering if there might be traces of the girl's DNA in Oliver's room or the basement or the woods by the house.

Runa and I also worried about the box of Gretchen's cremains. It looked like Oliver might have a lifetime supply of powder to use in resurrection rituals. Would that make him prone to more killings and raisings of the dead? We could only shudder at the thought.

I made up my mind that I would track that box down to the best of my ability during upcoming visits. I only hoped that Oliver hadn't distributed the contents to scores of sandwich baggies and hidden them around the house.

When our daughter was born, everyone descended on the hospital. I was drained, and of course Runa was exhausted after eighteen hours of labor. My family made it at the same time as Adele, and there were hugs all around. Everyone in my family, including my little brother, was crying. It felt great.

Adele was happy, but even more subdued than usual. I knew the reason why. She and I had talked a few weeks before, and this time we kept Runa out of the conversation in order not to freak her out.

Adele believed that Gretchen died before she'd had the opportunity to supervise the kids while they made individual efforts to resurrect the dead. Her illness drove the training into overdrive, but the end came too soon. Had she recovered, Gretchen likely would have set limits on them—brought them along gradually so that the ritualistic efforts were "age appropriate," whatever *that* means in this context. But that train had long left the station. These kids were raising the dead with abandon.

Adele was particularly concerned about the crazy shit that Oliver was up to. He had gotten it into his mind that all kinds of interesting stuff would happen if he distributed the ashes on top of things—like a pregnant woman—while performing the ritual.

She'll be back.

I shrugged this off, not willing to even go there.

After all the gasps and squeals over the new baby, my in-laws' excitement began to die down. Karla offered the baby back to me, and I sat by Runa's bed so we could stare at out little girl. Our daughter opened her eyes and whimpered. Everybody's heart melted, and there were some *awww*s.

"Look," Oliver announced to the entire room. Everyone turned their attention to the baby. "She has Grandma's eyes."

ANTHONY HAINS IS a professor emeritus of counseling psychology with a specialization in pediatric psychology. He retired in May 2018 after thirty-one years at the University of Wisconsin–Milwaukee. He has published five novels: *The Torment*, *Sweet Aswang*, *The Disembodied*, *Dead Works*, and *Birth Offering*. Anthony lives with his wife in Whitefish Bay, Wisconsin. They have one daughter.